Next Year In Paterson

Tales of the Great Assimilations

Ron Goldberg

ISBN: 979-8-218-65537-2

ACKNOWLEDGEMENTS

Many thanks to Aaron Berkowitz, Linda Bine, Glenn Kenny, Liza Murphy and Cliff Roth for their support and feedback, and to Larry Fishbein, Hal Gross and Steve Kramer for their recollections and camaraderie. Much gratitude also to Meghan Boots, Lew Brown, Brian Guyette, Harry Somerfield and Jennifer Swift, and a glass raised with the circle at Budafest; their memory has indeed been a blessing.

"Sink or Swim" was originally published by the Jewish Literary Journal, 2024

Cover illustration: "I and the City"
by Ron Goldberg and Meghan Boots

CONTENTS

For Brenda, my bashert

"Yet I will leave a remnant, that ye may have some that shall escape the sword among the nations, when ye shall be scattered through the countries."

Ezekiel 6:8

"It is not the strongest species that survive, nor the most intelligent, but the ones most responsive to change."

Charles Darwin

AUTHOR'S NOTE

In the years following World War II and peaking in the 1960s, the industrial city of Paterson, New Jersey, fifteen miles northwest of Manhattan, was home to over 30,000 Jews out of a population of 140,000; nearly a quarter of the city census. Many were descended from skilled European weavers who had arrived at the turn of the century and helped remake their new home into America's "Silk City." Many others were Holocaust survivors who settled there to live miraculous second lives among their kinsmen in the new world. By the approach of the new millennium, this entire community had vanished from the city, almost without a trace.

These works of fiction contemplate the arrivals and departures of this lost world. Resemblances to individuals living or dead are coincidental, with two exceptions. The New York City teachers' strike of 1968 was national news, and momentous enough to warrant actual voices, some of which can be heard through Miss Turner's cousin and on archival recordings still available via National Public Radio. Later in the collection, few readers will fail to recognize the late founder of the Jewish Defense League, whose philosophy has been quoted verbatim.

Paterson was America's first planned industrial center, founded by Alexander Hamilton to provide the "useful manufactures" needed by a modern, independent nation. The city powered the American ascent for a century and a half, contributing everything from the gun that won the west to the engine that launched the age of air travel.

Always a magnet for immigrants, some thirty languages are heard today in the city's school system. Hebrew and Yiddish are no longer among them. To hear those, you now go to the surrounding suburbs and further, where the various Orthodox communities live in numbers that would have raised the eyebrows of the Reform and Conservative Jews that helped build Paterson's golden age.

One day, another ethnic or religious group, speaking whatever language, will look back with nostalgia or relief at this same adopted city that they too have left behind. But the Jews can no more forget Paterson, and so many enclaves like it, than forget that they live in America. For them, the "old country" has a more contemporary geography.

• • •

NEVER FORGET

What was that, a rat? He hoped it wasn't but knew it was. Yes, of course it was a rat, and there are probably lots more down here, so try to ignore them and don't make a sound. Not that Sheldon had ever actually seen a rat to know what one really looked like. Not in the clean little house where he'd lived all of his seven years. God only knew what was happening there right now. Please God, he silently asked, let nothing be happening there.

He'd only seen a mouse there, only once. It was the night that Mitzi trapped a hapless straggler in the basement, too oblivious or complacent to sense obvious danger. He'd watched in frozen horror as the delighted tabby toyed with it at length. Over and again, with pitch-perfect sadism, she'd lift her paw and tease an escape, only to swat the ball of fur and blood back to its awful reality, as the shrieks grew louder and the will to survive grew fainter.

There could be no shrieking where Sheldon was crouched now, that was for sure. There could be only silence in this rat-friendly utility room. Above all, he had to remain dead silent. He knew that as much as he knew anything in this world. He hoped that his heartbeat, loud as a kettle drum in his ears, wouldn't give him away.

He was lucky, he thought, very lucky, to have seen and remembered the unlocked window to this hiding spot. Things had happened so quickly. Even though the whole city could feel the pressure, pushing down the air like a vise, no one really saw it coming. Not until it had finally combined and recombined the sums of its awful energies and birthed itself as a terrifying solid. He hoped the other kids were all right. Twelve-year-old David from up the block had left him in the schoolyard with the others. Just for a few minutes he said, and he'd be back with Dubble Bubble and a fresh Spaldeen from Smokey's Sweet Shop. But where was he now? Please God, he silently asked, let David be okay somewhere.

When the unmistakable sound of collective mayhem arrived within earshot, the kids bolted their separate ways like rabbits from a brushfire. For Sheldon, running all the way home from the schoolyard where they'd been playing that Sunday would have been well out of the question. Too far to go, too dangerous for sure.

Resourceful beyond his years and long adapted to many shades of fear, he hadn't panicked. He'd noticed earlier that a small basement window in the back of the school, hardly noticeable in its nook, had perhaps two inches of open gap, probably left for ventilation. While he knew there'd be no one inside on a Sunday that might protect him, he nonetheless sped back to the spot with no hesitation, with only the blind intuition that the tiny slit of open window was in fact, the main chance.

Easily reaching in to trip the long hook latch, he climbed down onto a grizzled wooden workbench and swung the window shut as best he could before quickly wedging himself below. Maybe nobody would look for him there, or even notice the window at all. He'd be safe here, maybe. At least for the moment. Outside, the noise was growing louder, closer, very close. Growling, vindictive voices, buzzing like a hornet's nest, punctuated by the arrhythmic clunk of a bat on asphalt. Baying in earnest for…what? Violence, destruction, and blood.

He'd often heard the warnings that this day would come. They'd arrive as hushed urgencies exchanged by the adults, mostly in Yiddish so that he would theoretically not understand and not be frightened. These sinister tidings seeped effortlessly from the family kitchen to the young boy's room and spelled danger like the distant howling of wolves.

From the darkness of his bed, he heard Uncle Saul and Aunt Julie practically beg his parents to up and leave Paterson, just as they had sped from Newark only a few months ago. The violence and destruction that roiled that aching city only last summer had taken as one of its casualties the tiny haberdashery that represented their entire security. The couple returned to their store the day after the riots to see the windows smashed and their decapitated mannequins pointedly arranged on the sidewalk. They felt no need for further clarification. Uncle Saul had been almost exactly Sheldon's age when his own parents had managed to leave Leipzig, almost exactly thirty years earlier.

There were others too that advised a speedy relocation. Why hadn't his parents listened? The Stadtfelds had moved away earlier this year too, not long after Josh had been caught in the wrong place at the wrong time. Caught by the same genus of multi-headed monster that Sheldon could hear out there in the rear of the schoolyard, right now, clear as day. They must be close by, he shuddered.

Poor Josh had ended up in the hospital with injuries that nobody ever named in detail. Naturally, these became the stuff of legend among the neighborhood boys, with ghastly speculations inspired by Chiller Theater. Sheldon's parents wouldn't even take him to visit his friend in the hospital. By the time Josh's rehabilitation was over, the Statdfelds' house was already on the market. Soon the family moved downstate, never to be heard from again.

How many of them were out there now, he wondered? How many people are there in a mob? Is twenty enough? Fifty? Is there something that's smaller than a mob but bigger than a gang? Whatever it's called, will they notice the slit in the window?

Startling another rat, Sheldon cautiously unfolded and craned, hoping to close any remaining gap in the window before anyone might see it. He saw there was no way he could climb up the table in time. Securing the window in the first place would have been much better, he cursed, what a tragic mistake. Why didn't he think of it immediately? Now he might not survive. Survival depends on thinking of things immediately. And on luck, of course, you always needed luck. Now he'd have to make himself invisible and pray for more luck. He shrank back under the table and tried to breathe as quietly as he could. Maybe they'll pass this spot. Maybe they won't notice the window. Maybe they won't see where he's hiding. Maybe the danger will go away.

But the danger never goes away. It just doesn't. Sheldon now understood, belatedly, that this ugly postulate must in fact be true; shockingly, horribly true, despite all his fervent efforts to deny its truth and safely believe it false. They were right after all, he gulped. The danger never goes away. It's always just around the corner, barely and imperfectly contained. And it could - no, would - appear at any time, such as right this minute. This core truth, now fully recognized as such, was the root and branch of his tree of knowledge, the elemental lesson, divulged over and over, in so many words and so many less, by the two haunted souls that had bequeathed his epigenetic fear and nurtured it like a hothouse flower: his survivor parents.

All right, so who could blame them? Those two knew fear like nobody else did, that much Sheldon knew must be true. Who could blame them, after all, if they wanted to be certain that their miracle child – tardily and surprisingly engendered here in America, under the iron grey skies of rusting Paterson, New Jersey, not fifteen years after the camps and the marches – was, and always would be, *absolutely* aware that the danger never goes away?

Had their English ever moved beyond the functional, they might even have phrased it that way. Instead the two of them, individually and together, spoke their own nuanced dialect of Holocaust impartation. In it, words were only guideposts, coarse indicators of meaning that broadly hinted at greater, unspeakable meanings deemed indescribable in words. The somber litanies of what happened to "us" and "your family," spoken of and hinted at so often, served through their repetition to create even more guideposts in the boy's mind, each newly and equally terrifying. By the time he was seven, his imagination of what lay beyond these markers was fully commensurate with their source material.

Were those hideous visions – the stuff of so many of the child's frequent nightmares – so much different than what was happening out there right now, not fifty feet away? Weren't they the same thing after all? They were still out there. He could still hear the growling, the cursing, the laughing that felt like the opposite of funny. He could sense the weirdly sour smoke that he'd sometimes smell behind the Carvel, where the bad older kids would gather in the evenings. None of them had ever bothered Sheldon or his pals before, as they happily marched to the counter and demanded a cherry bonnet. Why were they after us now? What did we do? Why are they so angry? Is it because we're Jewish? Not all of the kids in the playground were Jewish. How did they know who was?

It had been a punishingly hot spring. People were always in a worse mood with the temperature, that was for sure. Their bad moods multiplied when they came together and became something else, bigger than any of them, like that time Ruthie across the street accidentally burned the whole matchbook as she lit a Parliament. There are moments just like that matchbook, he thought, only with people.

It even happened before, not very long ago, when he was younger. He remembered it now. Race riots – that's what they called them in the Talmudically-observed Paterson Evening News – had broken out in the city during the summer when Sheldon was only four. Back then, his mother had barely concealed her anxious grief each day as his father left for his job in the drapery factory near the great falls, far from their safe Eastside neighborhood, eyeing her son frequently to make sure he was inside at best, outside the window at worst. Now, outside his own little window in the back on the school, the sounds of the monster were dissipating, but they had not yet vanished. Why aren't they leaving yet, he thought? And what are they so mad about? What did we do?

The city had had been nervous for days now. Somebody Arthur Luther King had been killed with a gun. Sheldon didn't know who he was, but he must have been important, it was even on TV. That mister King was right here in Paterson just last week and everyone seemed so happy, why did someone shoot him? Did Jews shoot him, is that why they're so mad at us?

And if they aren't mad at just us Jews, then how come it's always our Jewish friends who were moving away every year, to Fair Lawn and Glen Rock and even Wayne, in the parts where they're allowed? Sheldon wondered if he'd always have to live like this. How would he find new hiding places? He might not always be as lucky as he was this time. What if luck for people came in fixed quantities, like nine lives for cats, and today was the day when he'd emptied his share?

Until today, Sheldon hadn't pondered these questions for a long time. A long time for a seven-year-old might seem like small beer, but he'd made up his mind about these things in the second grade, upon entering public school. As far as he was concerned, that was a lifetime ago. He'd spent kindergarten and first grade at the city's sole remaining yeshiva, a move animated by pragmatism rather than piety, as both his parents needed to work, and no public school would enroll children younger than five. Sheldon ultimately begged them for the chance of attending "real" school like the other kids in the neighborhood. As soon as he got his wish, he breathed deeply in a way he had never known before. He'd been born again.

Children of every size, race, color, creed and religion populated his bustling classroom, laughing, jostling, all woven together as one tapestry, more or less, while a carousel of earnest teachers patiently intoned the day's lessons. It was like he had finally landed in America proper, the same place he saw on TV and in the movies, where nobody needed to speak in hushes. No matter that two years at the Khesed Academy had better prepared him to recite *Modeh Ani* than *I Pledge Allegiance*, or that he'd never seen cursive letters before, or even knew what science was.

It didn't matter. He was now in the real world. A world filled with living and breathing cousins and aunts and uncles and even grandparents. A world where everyone spoke English all the time and most often without accents, where adults laughed and drank homemade wine on their stoops while their teenagers stole kisses in dark corners and their youngest played on the curbs in front of their buildings, long after sunset. A world where people said sweet dreams to their children at bedtime.

With only a child's mind, he knew that his situation – his parents' situation – was special, even singular. He even knew that their tiny circle of friends, all of them survivors as well, were only that, just a tiny circle. And so it was with relief more than shock that from the first moments he entered the public sphere, through the buffed linoleum halls of P.S. 26, he saw with utter clarity that the world was much broader and brighter than the one explained by two undaunted but damaged refugees that had somehow made it through its most pitiless depths. There was another world out there and we live in it now, reasoned the boy. I live in it now. We are Americans. No, it won't happen here. This is America.

"*And where are you now, smart guy?*" asked all the voices inside him, piercingly, with the requisite accents. As he continued to scrunch into the smallest ball possible, Sheldon had to allow again that his parents must have been right after all. I guess it *can* happen here. It's happening right now, isn't it? Still? Are they still out there?

Cupping a hand to his ear as if it would make a difference (he had seen this bit of science in a cartoon), he warily judged that the sound of the crowd seemed to be gone at last. There was no more murmuring that he could hear, no more smoke smell; could it be they've moved on? He unfolded himself quietly, slowly, so as not to surprise any more rats. Climbing back onto the ancient utility table, caked with paint and turpentine, he peered out the crack of the window. There was nobody out there – nothing. Is this the moment? No, it was too soon. They might be around the corner. Better to wait.

Climbing down from the table, he gazed in awe at the mysteries of the utility room. He had never seen things like these in person. There were glass flasks and beakers, just like those in the Frankenstein movie his mother wouldn't let him watch, for fear of giving him nightmares. Sheldon was too young to appreciate such ironies. However, upon sneaking a viewing at his chum's apartment down the hall, he saw nothing nearly as frightening as the stuff of his highly explicit dreams. Especially the one where the bad men dressed in black break into the house and drag grandma and grandpa off and pitch them into a burning oven, where they would scream Sheldon's name until he woke up with a start.

Lately, this dream had stopped waking him. Maybe he had gotten used to it. Maybe he had begun to understand that it was only a dream, and who knew what those were anyway? Maybe he was the one that was right after all, and not his parents. The past is in the past, and what happened there would not – could not – happen here.

What else was on these huge shelves, so tall you needed a ladder to get to it all? He had never seen shelves so big, except for the day his mother took them downtown to get a library card for her avid young reader. She had brought him to the stately Paterson main branch, a landmark Classical Revival building by the architect who a few years later would design the Lincoln Memorial. Its grand staircase and imposing Ionian columns thrilled the boy to his core and convinced him more deeply of his evolving thesis, namely, that the world was surely a much bigger place than what he was led to understand at home.

There was nothing to be mad about with Mom and Dad, he reasoned. Or their friends for that matter, who would gather with them for company and rummy in quietly jolly get-togethers, where Polish, Hungarian, Romanian or Czech colored the Yiddish lingua franca, and English was something only occasionally barked at too-noisy children. No, the bleak warnings aren't their fault, Sheldon knew, they only want to protect me. It's their past that's doing the talking and who could blame them for that?

But they were wrong, he had decided long ago. They were just wrong. Now we're here and not there, and this is now, not then. One look up at the massive limestone pillars of the grand library, and the nearby statue of Alexander Hamilton, who had founded the city itself and had even been one of America's founding fathers, gave the boy inspiration and comfort. It was difficult, even wrenching, to disbelieve the worldview of one's own parents at such a tender age. But here, in stone and bronze, was something tangible and noble you *could* believe in. We're here in America, the best country in the world. It won't happen here.

Sheldon peered again through the crack of the window and felt sure that the bad men must be gone, but now he was transfixed by the utility room. One shelf had equipment for gym class. Imagine it Mom and Dad! Jews and Blacks and Irish and Italians and Puerto Ricans and Poles, Syrians, Greeks, Costa Ricans, Filipinos, even Germans – all playing games together! Stacked on another shelf were thick books containing wisdom he couldn't wait to uncover. Up there were goggles for boys that would learn to work a bandsaw; over there, gelatin molds to bore the girls in home economics.

Sheldon gaped at these wonders and dared to follow his curiosity out of the room, into an empty hallway. The deserted school looked celestial as the afternoon sunlight flooded every window it could find. He peered up at a trophy case filled with plaques and cups for outstanding achievements, dreaming that his own name would be up there too, one day. This is America, where everyone has a chance at achievement. Who knows how far he'll go? It's a big world out there, after all.

Flooded with unnamable emotions, Sheldon felt ready to leave the building and make his way home, hopefully without incident. He carefully closed the utility room door behind him and climbed back onto the table. Reaching up to open the window, crack by crack, he scanned the rear of the schoolyard and deemed it truly empty. He piled a few books on the table to help the climb, and in a moment, found himself standing in a faded hopscotch court, blessedly alone.

He immediately cursed himself for needing the books. The staff would find them there at some point, and even though nothing was stolen, they'd now know better than to leave this window unlocked in the future. That meant that this storeroom would no longer be a viable hiding place, should he ever need one again. But he wouldn't need one, he decided. The bad men were mad at something else, not at me, not at Jews, and probably the police have caught them already. Wherever they are now, they're no longer here.

This realization helped Sheldon's emotions unwind from high alert. His fear receded into its familiar corners, giving way to an analgesic flush of relief and then, remarkably, into something that he began to understand as pride. He had not panicked. He had saved himself. Maybe he could have tried to be a hero and tried to save the other kids, but maybe that wasn't needed after all. Maybe they all got home safely before the bad men saw them. And, anyway, survival isn't about saving others, it's about saving yourself.

That's one lesson he had learned cold from his mother, whose sister had been shot in the head right next to her for not keeping pace on the death march out of Auschwitz. She had managed to stifle her screams of horror and anguish and kept marching, and she had survived. And now, today, Sheldon knew that he was truly his parents' child. Today, he had survived. He now knew that he *could* survive. He now believed that he could confidently answer the unasked question that echoed through his still-evolving soul, and the souls of an entire second generation like him. He would have survived. Yes, he would have survived.

The streets near the chaotic 10th Avenue circle were eerily empty for a Sunday afternoon. The shops were largely closed, and as the city had been on tenterhooks for almost a week, the locals had wisely and overwhelmingly decided that on a hot day like this, there'd be no place like home. Sheldon had been well-taught to look both ways before crossing any streets, and as a careful boy, he did.

Luck may be a finite resource, as Sheldon had feared. Perhaps it really is apportioned in a single serving at birth or before, and spent, for better or worse, until the ration is gone, who can say? Or rather, luck might be a renewable, regenerating itself with each fresh expenditure, possibly inverting itself like a mirror with every incident, changing good luck for bad and vice versa. Maybe it's true that we make our own luck after all, or equally true that all outcomes are the work of the Lord. Luck has no lineage, no pattern or justice, no reason. It smiles on us with infinite mercy, or turns away with cold indifference, as it will.

While every building within two blocks surely heard the screech and the sickening sound of the skid, it was a long time before anyone came down to see if someone got hurt. When they did, no one was there.

• • •

MISS TURNER'S FIRST DAY

The second-floor hallway of P.S. 34 was nearing silence as the morning bell became a ghost. Most of the students had already fled to their classrooms, making this a solitary promenade to room 214, and a final few moments alone to gather her thoughts. It was a darling school, she thought, she'd like it here very much.

Crayoned posters commemorating Crispus Attucks Day lined the upper walls, showing exemplary enlightenment among these young children and even some artistic talent. As she continued down the hall, one entry in particular caught her eye. It was a surprisingly detailed illustration depicting the first martyr of the American Revolution, bleeding and dying on the ground, while two groups of onlookers hovered nearby. One was drawn with crude expressions of shock and agony over poor Mr. Attucks, a Black man rendered in burnt sienna, with mortal injuries in jagged swoops of scarlet. The other group leered with satisfaction at the outcome of the deed, though none of them actually held the musket.

She was excited to get started with these students at last, and looked forward to opening their young minds to everything, absolutely everything. She had waited for this day longer than expected. Having breezed through her coursework at Paterson

State Teacher's College, class of '68, and garnered nothing but sterling recommendations, an immediate position in a good school felt all but ordained, at least until the troubles started. But there was no time to think about that now. The time was finally here and her class would be waiting.

She opened the door of room 214 to the cacophony of twenty-seven fourth graders, laughing, cajoling, accusing and retorting, with the predictable accompaniments of spitballs, rubber bands and paper airplanes. Closing the door behind her, the noise stopped suddenly, as if someone yanked a cord. The children dashed to their seats, furtively glancing sideways before staring straight ahead with their most blameless expressions, hands folded neatly before them.

She strolled to the front of the room and, facing her class, smilingly introduced herself in a gentle contralto that pealed amiability and warmth, sensations that these children were not accustomed to at this hour, not from crabby and acerbic Mrs. Fisher. Wait, where was she? And who was this?

The lilting voice informed the room that "My name is Miss Turner." She turned to the chalkboard and in a clear, elegant script, wrote it for all to remember. "I'm looking forward to us learning together," she said, which sounded to the children like something secret and wonderful, a confidence. "So first I'd like to learn more about you. Let's begin by introducing yourselves. We'll start with A, of course. I think you're first, Susan Aaronson. You probably go first a lot," she smiled.

There was an uncomfortable pause before young Susan responded. It was as if the entire class hoped she'd answer for all of them. To greater or lesser degrees, all were now transfixed by the charming young woman perched jauntily on the edge of the teacher's desk. The children had returned from Christmas break prepared for those bleakest days of winter yet to come, which would be spent fearfully dodging Mrs. Fisher's unpredictable wrath and groaning to satisfy her militantly exacting ways.

Susan finally answered by raising her hand, which confused everyone, as she had already been called on to speak. "Yes, Susan?" The child answered shyly, "Is Mrs. Fisher okay? My mom heard from a friend of hers that she was sick."

The reply came in vividly reassuring tones that curled gracefully through the pin-drop silence. Its melody drew the children's attention rather than demanding it, sending yet another unfamiliar quiver through the room. "I'm afraid that's true, Susan. I can't say anything more about it because we should respect other people's privacy. We'll all talk more about privacy another time. But together, as a class, we'll send a nice get-well card to Mrs. Fisher. I know she misses you all."

"How long will you be our substitute?" asked Susan, energized at having instigated this important discussion. Smiling gently, Miss Turner answered, "I'm not a substitute, I'm your new teacher. What would make you think that I was a substitute?" The child shrunk visibly and turned crimson, murmuring that she didn't know. The silence resumed. The children remained transfixed and mute. They had never seen a Black teacher before.

*

Gloria Bethany Althea Turner, aged twenty-two, had known in advance that this would be the case. She was advised of it at length, both by those that fought for her to replace the ailing Mrs. Fisher and those who were steadfast against her. The former group had lobbied and more to fill the upcoming vacancy with a Black teacher, as P.S. 34 was one of the last remaining schools in the city to employ exactly none. They demanded, with uneven degrees of civility, that it was high time the school staff reflected its student body, which was decidedly more Black than its faculty.

The latter group of naysayers had nothing against this Miss Turner personally, and certainly nothing against her race, absolutely not. But there was such a thing as a teachers' union and also seniority, which Miss Turner did not possess, though many others did. To their minds, her hiring was nothing more than pandering and nothing less than illegal.

The tension had boiled over into Paterson from its original kettle in nearby Brooklyn, where many of the city's Jewish families could trace their roots. There, just months ago, in an atmosphere of white-hot emotions and distrust, some of which never dissipated, an epic battle had been waged between Black community leaders and the teachers' union, representing innumerable Jewish educators and administrators. Upon taking over their schools in the once-Jewish neighborhoods of Brownsville and Ocean Hill, the new Black leaders had summarily rid themselves of a number of Jewish teachers, attempting to transfer them to other districts, accusing them of obstruction, professional failure, and worse.

It would no doubt require many diverse experts to fairly assess the causes and effects of the 1968 Brooklyn teachers' strike, which became national news and produced acrimonies that often hardened into permanence. Suffice it to say that in nearby cities such as Paterson – undergoing many of the same transitions as its larger eastern neighbor – the conflict echoed with striking fidelity to the original. Which was to say, among the many other things to say, that the core issue of the kids' education became perhaps less mattering than who should be allowed to provide it.

When Miss Turner received the call from the school board informing her of her hire, there were few additional formalities. Her orientation manual arrived by courier the next day. She had already toured the school during her interview, which was held in the evening after everyone had gone home. It had been surprisingly cursory: a brief read-through of her achievements and references, obligatory questions about herself and her ambitions, including thoughts of motherhood.

Gloria assured them of the seriousness of her professional outlook. She had come from a long line of teachers in the Turner family and was committed to education and children, with no plans for any of her own (at least for now, she thought). Satisfied with these answers, the interviewers shook her immaculately manicured hand and wished her the best of luck. One of the board members caught her arm on the way out and sheepishly apologized for the "noise" surrounding her hire. Another followed her all the way out to her car and made fumbling small talk before asking for a date.

*

The lunch recess was nearly over, and on the asphalt and glass-shard grounds of P.S. 34, Miss Turner's fourth-grade students were huddled in pockets to discuss their new situation.

Leonard Rosen was the first to say anything against her, murmuring theatrically that she was nothing but a token. When pressed to define this unfamiliar epithet, which sounded unambiguously insulting, he muttered that he couldn't say exactly. However, his uncle was overheard grumbling that the schools were being forced to hire token "colored," and since he was a teacher himself, who would possibly know better? A piccolo voice suggested that we should ask Miss Turner what the word means, but this was quickly shushed down by the others.

Daniel Weissman cleared his throat, and assuming the mediating aspect that would one day land him a judge's robe, soberly reminded the group that we don't know anything yet. We only know there's been a change.

In a nearby cluster, Miss Turner's Black fourth graders were gathered together, nearly all of them, smiling broadly or quizzically, but smiling nonetheless. They'd overheard their parents talk about how Black teachers had taken charge of some schools in New York, but never thought they'd see that here. Not in this neighborhood, why would they? But now they were collectively feeling the first tingles of a strange new euphoria.

This unfamiliar sensation undoubtedly owed much to the one-of-us affirmation now visible at the head of their class. But at the same time, their excitement heralded a dawning sense of a broader liberation. A possible liberation, anyway – a liberation at last – from the teacher's subtle frowns and hurtful sighs, and the class-wide humiliations when you don't have the right answer. How come mean Mrs. Fisher never picks on the white kids huh? Maybe they don't know the answer neither. But Irene Lewis always knows the answers, and so does Donald Douglas. How come she never calls on them? They're just as smart as the Jew kids. Maybe now things will finally start to go the other way.

At the sound of the bell, grades four through six were ushered into the wooden auditorium for one of the school's semi-monthly assemblies. Old Mrs. Watchman took her accustomed spot at the chipped Sohmer upright, while Mr. Kanter adjusted the microphone stand for petite Mrs. Brownstein, who strode purposefully to the stage and quieted the children with well-worn arm motions. She had been teaching at this school for twenty-one years, witnessing much change, and recently wondering how much longer she'd be able to keep it up. Or whether she'd be allowed to keep it up, she sighed to herself. It had been a rewarding career for Nettie Brownstein, with many deep satisfactions, but she had lately begun to intone the mantra of re-election campaigns, thinking frequently about four more years, four more years.

Clearing her throat, she addressed the room. "Boys and girls, as you know, this week we are honoring the memory of – who? – that's right, *Crispus Attucks*. Not everyone knows that the first man to give his life for the War for Independence – which gave us our American freedom – was a Negro. But we know better, don't we?" The children responded in the affirmative, with varying levels of volume and pitch.

"And it's important for us to also know that right now, we Americans are at a moment of wonderful, historic change in our country," she continued. "Just four years ago, our President signed a big new law called the Civil Rights Act, which guarantees that all Americans, no matter who they are, no matter what race or creed or religion, gets a fair chance. And only a few months ago, they made that law even stronger. Thanks to the new Fair Housing Act, it's against the law to treat people unfairly when they go to look for a home. They can't be treated differently because of the color of their skin."

She smiled with approval at this abrupt ending of race prejudice, which had been rendered completely extinct by legislative decree. Oh well, she knew she'd oversimplified the situation, but these were fourth graders after all. She was proud to have personally favored such legislation, and of the contribution that Jews had made in bringing it about. "It's so silly and it doesn't make any sense," she soothed. "Prejudice against people for something as silly as the color of their skin. Some people have white skin, some have brown, or red, or yellow. Underneath we're all the same people. Aren't we?" As one, with only a few abstentions, the children answered, "Yes, Mrs. Brownstein."

*

Gloria Turner had been mulling this same question with unexpected frequency over the past few weeks. She wholeheartedly believed in the same answer, that we are all the same people underneath. Regrettably, that meant the bad as well as the good found in people everywhere, in many she knew and many more she didn't.

From the day she was first contacted as a potential replacement for the ailing Harriet Fisher, she'd pretty much heard it all. More than all. From both sides. From all sides. From too many sides. It made her head hurt and her heart ache. With each passing day there'd be another blow from someone. You're in the right. You're in the wrong. You're a hero. You're a traitor. You're a role model. You're a Tom. Her spirit jerked back and forth according to these voices, wreaking hurtful confusions of every kind, as the political football that she had unwillingly become was punted back and forth in an ugly contest between two sides grimly determined that the other must not win.

It began innocently enough, in conversation with a former classmate over eggs and Taylor ham at the Madison Plaza Diner. Her friend Dolores Hayes had not yet received a teaching offer since graduating with Gloria from Paterson State. She had quickly gotten a tryout as a student teacher in one of the city's more challenging schools, but had found herself flummoxed by its aggressive disruptions and unable to establish any authority or rapport. The unruly and sometimes even lewd sixth graders exploited these failures with tireless energy, and by the end of the marking period, Dolores was no longer sure that education was her calling.

Still, Dolores had earned her certification and done well at it too, not to mention that her family had pinched themselves to put her through school. She'd be patient. She knew better than to waste time applying to nearby suburban districts like Hawthorne, Haledon or Fair Lawn. There's no way they'd hire her, she thought. Not with her complexion, not with her hair. For goodness' sake, there were still schools in Paterson itself with no Black teachers at all – like the one her friend Gloria Turner was now cheerily describing at the table.

Staring down at her coffee cup, Dolores hid her unsettling mix of surprise, delight and disappointment as she listened to her friend's news. She was only mildly surprised that old P.S. 34 was finally taking in a Jackie Robinson at this late date, and mildly pleased that it would at least be Gloria, who was such a wonderful person and would make such a fine teacher.

Her tinge of disappointment came from the icepick sense that of course such a position would go to someone light-skinned and pretty like Gloria, not dark and plain, as she was. Maybe never dark and plain like she was, maybe never at all for that matter, Lordy, she thought. You had to look like Diahann Carroll like on that TV show about the nurse. That's what they like, that's what they feel comfortable with. That's what Gloria looks like; in fact, *she looks just like her*, everyone thinks so.

Dolores processed all of this and more into her most presentable smile before asking, "Sister, that is the whitest school in the city. Are you really going to be happy teaching snotty Jewish kids instead of your own people?"

On the opposite pole, Gloria's parents had been delighted with her instant decision to accept the position at P.S. 34, even though they knew the subtle and not-so-subtle tests that lay ahead. She was grateful for their unwavering support, because others in her world were less unconditional. Many of them had been thrilled by the gains that local Blacks had seemingly achieved in those Brooklyn school communities. That similar changes might now come to Paterson was a thought that swiftly advanced from wistful to hopeful.

Some from the community urged advancement that was swifter still, beyond hopeful, into active expectations and demands. This was especially true of Ricky Jenkins, Gloria's cousin, who had lately taken to wearing dashikis and calling himself Ashante X. In gospel cadences that shuttled between outrage and pathos, he bluntly informed Gloria that by teaching in a school that was majority white, she would merely be perpetuating her own people's oppression. She'd be teaching Black kids to act white, to go off like dumb, submissive lambs into a world where they had no place, all while prostituting herself as a house Negro (though described in more pungent terms).

"We proved it in Brooklyn," Ricky thundered with fierce pride. "We took back our schools in our communities, despite the kicking and screaming from the damned Jews and their damned kike teachers' union trying to destroy us with their miseducation. With the white man's education. We showed that we can do it for ourselves. We can teach our own what it is to be our own Black, beautiful selves. We need educators – yeah, I'm talking about *you*, girl. The system has been limiting our education for too long, keeping us from getting jobs and keeping us in slums. We need to fight for our full self-determination. It's the only way we'll gain our dignity and liberation."

With more hurt than agitation, Gloria asked how such a noble goal would be better served by the symbolic act of her refusing to teach in a changing school where a third of the students were already Black…this year.

Ricky gave a long, low whistle at the logic of her defense. "Girl, you need to open your mind," he drawled. "You need to know what time it is."

*

Over on the east side of the city, where Miss Turner's students lived, the news of her first day landed with mixed feelings. Surprise, dread and resignation were chief among them. The city's most deeply Jewish neighborhood had been closely following the coverage of the Brooklyn strike, the more sordid details of which had inflamed their ire as well as their fears, and had broken a piece of their hearts.

"And we've been such good friends to them, the *schvartzes*," hissed Mrs. Faltmeyer as she served the family dinner. "You see where it gets you. One day we're being murdered in a swamp for helping them vote, the next day they're on the radio saying they wish we were dead."

Between forkfuls of boiled flanken, Mr. Faltmeyer asked his wife to please tone it down at the table, while young Leonard Faltmeyer asked if they really wanted us dead. It didn't feel like Miss Turner did, she seemed nice.

"Oh, I'm sure she's very nice. But believe me, there are people behind your nice teacher that wouldn't mind seeing us dead. Or at least gone from here. And they'll get what they want. Soon there will be an exile, we'll all leave from here, and then there will be no more Jewish teachers to try to educate their *farzeenishe kinder*. Let them teach each other, *gay gezunter heit*."

Other parents on the Jewish eastside didn't know what to feel. Poor Harriet Fisher, a friend and neighbor with late stage cancer, had been a teacher at P.S. 34 for as long as they could remember. That she would one day be succeeded (never replaced!) by one of the smart neighborhood girls was an assumption that was easy to make and difficult to drop. Many of the Eastside daughters were teachers themselves, and many others were active as part-time substitutes. Surely one of them, whomever had the seniority and the best credentials, would be filling poor Harriet's place. This slice of the city had always been Jewish and was still largely Jewish, and we're not in Brooklyn (thank God!) where they need police to wedge themselves between us and them in front of the children at school.

One of the local girls had graduated with Gloria Turner and said she knew her personally as a lovely person. "She'd be a wonderful teacher anywhere," said Debra Litvin. "I just don't know why it has to be here. There are plenty of other schools that need her. I guess if it has to be someone like her, it might as well be her. I mean I liked her as a person."

"That's the problem," countered Arlene Wolff. "What I mean is she's not the problem, and that's the problem. They just wanted a Negro teacher and that's that. It doesn't matter who she is, she might as well be someone else, who cares, as long as she's also a Negro. And even *that* doesn't matter, because that's not the problem either! The problem is that there were others in line for that job that earned it and deserved it. All this time I thought they said they didn't want to be treated differently because of the color of their skin."

Debra's drew breath for a reflexive retort, but the words never took shape. They were all confused. Angry and confused.

Scattered among these troubling voices, Gloria did find occasional spots of light and affirmation. She visited the old college campus to thank her two favorite mentors, both of whom thrilled to her news. Starchy Mrs. Vandersloot, known on campus as "Ironskirt" and rarely seen to crack a smile, even went so far as to remove her lapel pin and present it as a gift. It was a small silver brooch with a cross and the name of Jean Baptiste de La Salle, whom she explained as the patron saint of teachers. Gloria kept this memento forever in the deepest reaches of her jewel box.

When she arrived home later that day, next-door neighbor Eunice Chester warbled congratulations from the upstairs window and invited Gloria in to celebrate with a slice of her famous pecan pie. At her humble table, she told Gloria how proud she was, because she never had much education when she was a girl. "There wasn't much of it to git" where she grew up in North Carolina.

"When I heard you'd be teaching those kids my heart near busted wide open," she sang. "I want you to promise me that you'll be teaching every last one of them to be as much of a lady as my baby girl Gloria from next door turned out to be. I'm so proud of you, child." From that day forward, every taste of pecan pie nearly brought tears to Gloria's eyes.

Another snapshot from those same heady first days at school stayed with Miss Turner for the rest of her teaching life, which went on for a quarter of a century. It happened on day one as she vainly searched the hallways for a storage room that was rumored to have an unused globe. Rounding a corner, she passed Mr. Robinson the janitor, who everyone in the school knew as Freddy, as he pushed a large trash container. They shared brief, friendly eye contact, but when after a few steps she realized she was in the wrong place again, she noticed that he was still motionless at the other end of the hallway, gazing back at her. She smiled and approached him. He shyly stepped forward, not wanting to speak so near the trash.

In a quiet voice that was audibly accomplished at being quiet, he said, "Hello there ma'am, I just wanted to come over and say welcome. My name's William Robinson but everyone here just calls me Freddy. If there's anything I can do for you, anytime, you just let me know, and I'd be glad to help. So happy to see you here, um hmm. Sure is nice to see another face with some color!"

He was perhaps twice her age, or maybe three times. He reminded her of Uncle Julius, who had been a Pullman porter back in the '40s and even worked for a time with "Detroit Red" on the old New Haven line. She reached out to shake his hand, which he wiped before accepting hers. She smiled sheepishly and asked, "Well Mr. Robinson, if you can point me to storage room D, I'd certainly appreciate it."

He beamed, "It's just down the end of that hallway to the left, Miss. And you can call me Freddy." She turned toward the correct hallway with a song in her heart, one that was repeated endlessly on the radio these days. Remembering that she hadn't thanked him, she turned to face him, raised an imaginary glass in the air, and smiling broadly, gave a toast: "*And here's to you, Mr. Robinson.*" Freddy couldn't remember the last time he was addressed as such.

*

By the end of the school year, Miss Turner had won the hearts of the children and even her co-workers. There was no doubting her classroom results. There were higher grades and fewer absences, and as her evaluators made note of her magnetism and can-do spirit, they congratulated themselves on having made a brilliant hire – in spite of the pushback from the community, who even remembered it now?

Those on the Eastside who were crestfallen at this turn of events stared unblinkingly at their changing city. Their sons looked outward into the suburbs and the metropolis, and their daughters sought unmarked worlds beyond the teaching and nursing that had marked the previous boundaries of received expectations.

As for the rest of the city, based on these and other shifting winds, many other Miss Turners would soon follow Gloria at P.S. 34 and other schools of the district. But for now, in the last sweltering days of June before the long-awaited summer break, the original model was handing out the year's final report cards.

When the last bell of the year struck, most of the children bolted from the room; but a handful lingered, waiting for the others to leave. These included Steven Katz, who would one day design educational software based on associative concepts he learned in Miss Turner's class, and Jodi Bernstein, who became only the second woman to perform open heart surgery in the history of the state of New Jersey. Steven and Jodi together thought they were an item, insofar as their ages understood the term. They approached Miss Turner's desk almost as a married couple.

"We just wanted to say goodbye to you," said Jodi. "And thank you for everything," added Steven. "You were the best teacher I've ever had." "Oh, me too," chimed Jodi. "The best teacher we ever had. We're going to miss you so much." Miss Turner could barely keep her watering eyes hidden behind her broad smile. "But this isn't goodbye," she bravely chirped. I'll be back here in the fall and so will you. You'll probably be in Mrs. Hirschman's class, the two of you."

"No," answered Steven, "We're moving away...I mean, my family is moving this summer. "Ours too," Jodi added, "We're going to miss Paterson so much! And you too! We won't see you again, so we wanted to say goodbye."

• • •

THE GOLEM OF 29TH STREET

Part One

Adam's parents met during a ski weekend in Vermont, a trip that his mother had earned through exceptional grades during this, her final year at the Orange Memorial Hospital School of Nursing, class of 1958. Her parents had been so delighted with her scholastic performance that they almost didn't ask if there would be boys on this trip. After all, a nurse as smart and personable and pretty as Miriam would have no trouble attracting a nice young doctor sooner than later anyway. This venerable theory would have no doubt proven true had Miriam not met Marcel, the ski instructor.

She found him incredibly handsome and, as if under a spell, could barely look away throughout the entire weekend. She'd never met anyone like him before, a real "outdoor" man, she thought, radiant in his wind-blown ruddiness and possessed of a remarkably rich, virile voice that descended near basso profundo.

It was Marcel's bottomless voice, which still carried more than a trace of the Quebecois French he'd grown up with, that had served up Cupid's deadliest arrow. As he gently instructed her on the slope and flirted après ski at the fireplace, Miriam swayed with emotions she'd never felt before. His voice went through her in the way she thought morphine must feel to the patient. It produced vivid sensations of an intoxicatingly warm space, safe and comforting. A place blissfully free of anxiety and pain.

Miriam knew enough about morphine from school to understand that it was dangerous to try and highly addictive. Despite this knowledge, she felt no remorse in leaving the other girls and slipping out of the room for a rendezvous with Marcel during her last night at the lodge. He approached her through the snow-covered darkness as if from a dream and led her to an empty cabin. There they made love over and over in a haze of perfect coupling that both knew would mark a pinnacle of their experience, a night that neither would ever forget. They were prescient in this assumption because a few weeks later, Miriam missed her time of the month.

In those days, nice girls like Miriam weren't supposed to have lovers, much less the complication of an unplanned pregnancy, among other impending complications. She certainly had not expected anything so extra-curricular on her ski trip and would have likely applied the brakes to Marcel after some heavy petting, had he not unwrapped a small blue package of Fourex at the pitch of their excitement and adroitly sheathed himself with lambskin. While this was not Miriam's first time with a man, she had still limited experience with the precautions incumbent upon these matters. The last man – boy really – had awkwardly promised to pull out before there'd be trouble, a declaration that did little to set a romantic mood and in fact simply provided cover for what diplomacy might call an early exit.

The fact that Marcel had come prepared in this way oddly spoke to Miriam's overdeveloped sense of responsibility, even in a moment of incandescent passion, when responsibility speaks only in faint whispers. This man had thought about it, thought about her, and hadn't left the responsibility up to her, she mused, before closing her mind and giving herself over to the moment. This man was a *mensch*. He cared enough to protect her. That the protection ended up failing that night wasn't his fault, Miriam would say for the rest of her life. It was God's will.

Marcel was a veteran of many ski weekends and many young women at the lodge, and frankly regarded their clockwork renewals as a fair component of his compensation. That said, the sameness of these assignations grew shopworn over time, and their aimless character laid the groundwork for the profound impact that Miriam would have on him, virtually at their first words.

Just what it was about her that had moved him so immediately and deeply, re-animated him even, he couldn't clearly say, even years later. She seemed to him an improbably friendly visitor from the larger civilization to which he did not belong, from the cosmopolitan places of complexity and genius that lay distant beyond the Green Mountains, beyond his experience and probably his reach.

She was so utterly different from the blowsy coeds that giggled down the bunny slope, or perhaps at him, or the local girls that sniffed at his accent and meager prospects. Here was a proud daughter from the unvisited worlds of faceless crowds and imposing buildings, who, despite her ineffably superior gifts, was nonetheless speaking to him with obvious attraction, and thrilling him on the slope with words he'd never heard before, like hypothermia and equilibrium.

While Marcel's routes toward the empty cabins were nothing if not well-traveled, he led Miriam to Mohican 4A with a physical nervousness he hadn't experienced since boyhood. When both were about to finally entwine, her infinitely accepting eyes dissolved this anxiety like frost under sunlight, which sent Marcel into a euphoric state that left his emotions shuddering long after he had led her back to her room.

*

When her time of the month was tardy enough, Miriam discreetly validated her fears with a sympathetic intern who was a friend of a friend, and debated how she would handle all this. As a nurse in training, she had a relatively clear idea of her options, illicit as they would have to be. But as a young woman who was deeply inside of an infatuation that yearned to call itself love, she wasn't willing to consider them, not yet.

She had wanted – expected – a child for as long as she could remember, with the certainty that she would one day be as loving and nurturing a mother as she would be a wife, and would repay her beloved parents for the gift of her own life with the reciprocal gift of grandchildren.

Thinking about things in this seemingly logical way, everything all seemed so beautiful and right, despite the storm clouds that lay ahead with said beloved parents. Their coming heartbreaks would need more than one hand to count: promiscuity, pregnancy, scandal, adoption maybe, a secret termination maybe, a shotgun wedding maybe, to someone only God knows who, probably not even Jewish.

Improbably, this last heartbreak struck Miriam out of nowhere. Not that her family could be called observant by any means, but it was certainly Jewish through and through. The topic of intermarriage was never discussed because in all the years of the Feldstein family circles of Paterson, it had simply never come up. What were the chances that Marcel was Jewish?

Miriam chuckled at the absurdity and suddenly remembered the silver crucifix around his neck; she had never had occasion to touch one before. She remembered his eyes as she fingered it. They seemed so vulnerable and quizzical, and in truth they were, because at that very moment Marcel realized that he was in bed with a Jewess, which would have been the first time, to his knowledge.

There were few role models for single mothers back in that day, as Miriam would recount years later. Beyond the social and familial stigmas, there were pragmatic concerns over her future in the medical profession: as a nurse at least, maybe even more one day. Yet she could not, for more than an instant, seriously consider the alternative to having the baby. Besides, she knew what the other girls in the neighborhood knew: that the alternative meant a clandestine trip to a back room upstairs at Glickman's drug store, where these covert solutions were practiced with varying degrees of sanitation, skill and secrecy.

No, she wanted the baby and already felt cosmically connected to its father; she wanted him too. But she knew that if she were to go down this path there was much to do, and she'd have to act sooner than later. She used a pay phone to place a long-distance call to the Stowe Maiden Lodge and left a message for the ski instructor Marcel, asking for a number where he could be reached. By the afternoon she had a number, and that evening she placed what was the most momentous call of her life, at least up until that time.

"Do you remember me?" she asked, without a greeting or saying her name. "Of course yes," he replied with gentle truthfulness, in the voice that went through her even over the wire. "I...been thinking about you...a lot," he confessed.

Taking a deep breath, she said "I'm very glad to hear that. I've been thinking about you too. I'd like to see you again, but you're a long way from me. I wonder if we could meet in the middle? I could take a train to Albany, and I have a friend there who has an apartment where we could meet. It's halfway between where…"

"Yes, I would come," he said, without letting her finish.

The following Friday, both lied to their respective responsibilities with a sick day and took the train to Albany. They did indeed meet in her friend's apartment, but not for a reprise of Mohican 4A. While their reunion kiss immediately recalled all the electricity of that first night, Miriam nevertheless sat him down and got straight to the business at hand.

She honestly didn't know how he would react, and elated probably would been her last guess. When Marcel finally understood that Miriam wanted to keep the baby and moreover keep him too, his eyes welled with the first tears of joy he had ever felt. As the couple finally embraced, they marveled at their own craziness, but at the same time astonished themselves for their bravery and certitude.

They could make it together. They would make it work. There was such a thing as love at first sight. One's bashert might come from anywhere. They weren't a bird and a fish. They were complementary halves of a single cosmic whole that had magnetically and poetically repaired itself through fate, chance, or whatever illuminates the brighter side of the universe. They sealed their future together with transcendental lovemaking that seemed to go on for centuries.

*

The first time Marcel came to meet Miriam's parents, anxieties were at the cusp of boiling. It had taken many sessions of familial wailing to get to this point, the general tenor of which should be obvious enough. Herb and Betty Feldstein had always stood behind their admirable daughter in all her life's decisions, which until now had always been uncannily sound. It was only in this knowledge that they were eventually able to relent from their opening stance of outrage and disbelief, and move through subsequent stanzas of hurt, anxiety, cajoling and dire warnings, before finally landing in exhaustion at resigned acceptance. Miriam was a sensible girl after all and had always been wise and mature beyond her years. Maybe it will all work out for the best, they thought. We look forward to meeting him, they said.

Marcel had washed and borrowed his family's snow-pitted Rambler for the 300-mile journey from Vergennes to Paterson. In the days before President Eisenhower's highway bill finished churning its way to the very top lid of the country, the ride meant many endless patches of meandering two-lane farm roads. Save for a holiday trip with his high school pals over the border to Montreal, intended as a sort of Rumspringa but remembered mostly for a bar fight that cost him a broken molar, Marcel had never driven further from home than the Burlington train station. As a result, it took him nearly twelve hours to reach the Feldstein residence, a stretch through which he had been continually and thoroughly terrorized by the unfamiliarities of speed, traffic and urbanity.

The evening, once it finally commenced, could not reasonably be called a success. Despite everyone's best efforts, Miriam's parents were predictably underwhelmed by their prospective son-in-law, and for the first time ever, disappointed in the child that had never disappointed them before.

They were glad to be able to hide these thoughts behind the sturdier objections of how, exactly, Marcel intended to support Miriam and their baby, a question to which Marcel had already given much fruitless thought. It was laughable to think she'd live on love as the poor wife of a rural ski instructor, freezing in winters, starving in summers, a city nurse in a place where some doctors still made house calls by horseback and took their fees in poultry. Her not speaking any French either, and that was bad enough, but not even Catholic besides. No, he would have to come to her, be one of her world, *merde*, let those ships fall wherever they are going to sail, he thought.

He confidently told Herb and Betty, as he had already told Miriam, that he knew his way around a textile mill, there being many in his part of New England. He had heard that Paterson was a big place for textiles, the Silk City eh? He would find a living for them there. There would always be opportunity for a skilled hand like his. "Because people," he said, in the seductive bass register that had so moved their daughter, "they're always going to need the clothes, and the textiles is what makes the clothes possible."

The veracity of this humble observation seemed self-evident to all, and even spurred Mr. Feldstein to bravely quip that his new son-in-law might have a *yiddishe kup* after all. The fact that Marcel's claimed work experience was in no way factual did not prove evident or consequential until later, and by then it didn't matter so much.

Marcel's own forebears had immigrated as poor dairy farmers from Quebec to become slightly less poor dairy farmers in Vermont, and had arrived in America in the same year that Herb Feldstein's grandfather landed at Ellis Island. As he grew up, Marcel's family never paid him a great deal of mind. More precisely, they paid as much mind as one might imagine to the fifth of seven sons in a family of thirteen children. Certainly, his parents were happy when his undeniable talent on skis resulted in gainful employment at the local lodge. This never overcame their regret that his muscular hockey skills, always the terror of the local boys, had not resulted in an even more gainful pro contract. Fortunately, this family hope for a ticket out of poverty was easily transferred to his two younger brothers.

When his parents had fully absorbed this lunacy about marrying one of the *filles laches* from the lodge, they smiled and wished their boy well, but were saddened to know that he'd be leaving Vergennes and going off to not-even-he-knows-where-yet. Still, there was nothing else for it. There was going to be a baby and never any question of any other way, and at least you can now skip the Pre-Cana, eh? That their son was to bring a Jew into their family was not an altogether kosher topic as it were, for these rustic practitioners of *la revanche des berceaux*. Their advice was simple, as they were proud, simple people: "Son, bring her into the church if you can and good luck to you, because as everyone knows, *les Juifs* are stubborn devils. But above all, be sure to raise your son (and they wished him a son) a good Catholic."

*

Adam was born, aptly enough, near midnight on a lightning-filled October night. For many years, his mother joked that it was like giving birth in a horror movie on Halloween. The blessed event arrived some seven months following the simple civil wedding that Miriam's parents had arranged and had cried throughout, not solely for the happy reasons these occasions generally merit.

For their part, Marcel's parents sent regrets, good wishes and a bolt of lace that had been in the family for many generations. "We are an ancient people like you," he informed his new in-laws, "some of the oldest in the new world." After City Hall, the Feldsteins hosted a family-only reception in their small home near Eastside Park. Their new son-in-law declared it as beautiful a house as any he had ever seen, an assertion Mr. Feldstein sadly thought was probably true. Nonetheless, Miriam smiled beatifically throughout the entire affair and glowed in anticipation of her charmed life to come. Despite every challenge she knew she was about to face, she remained optimistic, and on this, her big day, was unshakably cheerful.

In the months leading up to Adam's entry into the world, Miriam took charge of their future with leadership that was spectacular even to those that knew her best. Her father, who graciously helped with the rent, also helped Marcel find a job at the mills, which in the days before the great rusting had always accepted with alacrity all the help they could find, with few questions asked. Uncle Sy helped find a cheap apartment close enough for Marcel to walk to work at the North Star Silk and Dye Works. On quiet nights, the couple fell asleep to the lullaby drone of the majestic Paterson Falls, as one might hear the ocean in the distance.

After filling her husband's daily lunchbox, Miriam would walk to the first of three buses to get to school, which she was determined to complete – with honors – in time for class graduation and well ahead of her due date. With all this, she still managed, in her condition, to make meals and make love, to do the shopping and cleaning and find time to study. As stressful as these months were, Miriam looked back on them fondly for the rest of her life. She often told her young son that those hard months before he was born are what made her so strong, and that's why her darling boy grew up to be so strong too. Adam cooed with delight the first time he heard this story as an infant, and smiled with remembrance and tenderness the last time he heard it, many years later, as his mother lay peacefully in hospice care.

Histrionics of weather notwithstanding, Adam's entry into the world was thankfully uneventful. He was, at nearly ten pounds, a strapping boy from the start, but mother and child came through the event quickly and easily, and the expectant father had barely begun a fresh pack of Luckies when the waiting room nurse bluntly informed him of a son.

When the doctor slapped Adam to inaugurate his existence, the boy took the violence personally. As best he could, he fixed his slit newborn eyes with something that might almost be a glare, and the first cry out of his tiny mouth wasn't one of shock, fear, or pain, but something in the key of anger. This strange exchange lasted only a second and passed without notice from the busy doctor or exhausted mother. But even though he was never really conscious of it, Adam never forgot it.

*

As Adam grew up, his doting mother was always happy to talk about anything, but there was one story that Miriam never shared with him. It happened long ago, the night of his father's very first visit from Vergennes to Paterson, when the family's blessing over the couple's plans was far from assured.

Immediately following the brisket dinner, which was served late and in patches of silence, Miriam suddenly announced that she and Marcel would be taking a drive around the neighborhood. Grabbing her coat swiftly enough to arouse curiosity, if not suspicion, she glibly explained the outing as a useful sightseeing tour of Marcel's new hometown. As it was quite dark out by now and even a bit rainy, the alibi thudded weakly, without further comment. As the couple scurried out the door, Herb and Betty reluctantly added deceit to the list of their daughter's surprising and lamentable new qualities.

For a while, the couple drove aimlessly up and down Broadway, as Miriam alternated between tour guide and post-game analyst. She felt the evening had gone at least as well as it could have, but Marcel's furrowed brow and grunted assents dampened her cheer, and soon she was as deep in silence as he was. Suddenly, he pulled the car over to an open curb and killed the engine.

Looking into her eyes with his utmost intensity, he said, slowly and carefully, with great emphasis, using the voice that he knew she loved so much, "I want to be a Jew for you. I would change myself to a Jew for you."

Miriam returned his stare with some surprise. Because she was not at all religious – who was anymore? – she presumed that he wasn't either, and for the most part, she was right, as always. Years later, when it no longer mattered, Miriam better understood that she hadn't given much weight to what Marcel would be giving up in order to achieve this momentous plan. She had only thought of what she would gain. And as she added it all together, in that one specific moment, she perceived that gain as a dishonest offering.

It would be something that would be done only for show. For nothing, really. He wasn't Jewish and never really would be, even if some rabbi said he was on a piece of paper. It would be silly to perform this pantomime for the sake of – what exactly? The baby would be Jewish because she was Jewish, that much was true. So what if the father wasn't?

Was the fact that Marcel wasn't Jewish – and arguably some antonym thereof – part of her attraction? In her youthful inexperience, Miriam had not considered this possibility. But the naked truth of it was that somewhere deep inside herself, in corners she didn't often visit, she'd always harbored mixed and confusing emotions about her identity, or religion, or bloodline, or whatever it was that had bound her, without anyone asking, to the chosen people.

These feelings, when they occasionally jelled into actual thoughts, were generally soothed by the simple dictum that tradition was good for tradition's sake. She had dutifully sat through Sunday and Hebrew school on those terms. She was proud to be one of the first girls in her neighborhood to come of age with a public Bat Mitzvah. She loved the high holy days of course, the only days of the year when the Feldsteins would decamp for the synagogue. But in truth, she loved them to see this year's new babies and everyone's new clothes, and hear all about the engagements and college acceptances, while autumn chestnuts fell from the red and orange trees in the afternoons before the lovely family repasts. All of that was very beautiful indeed. She saw no reason why any of it would have to change now.

Lately though, with quiet stealth that gained momentum through each new step into the larger adult world, these less-examined sides of Miriam's least-examined emotions demanded greater audience. They leached through her innocence and the psychic insulation that Herb and Betty had always done their best to protect her with, as the rest of the extended family circle had always protected their own children, as the entire Jewish community of Paterson and beyond had protected themselves and their loved ones from time immemorial.

Because her hometown had long been a city of so many immigrants, with an improbable hodge-podge of races, creeds, ethnicities and nations jammed in roughly counterbalancing numbers, the baser displays of outright bigotry were not usually out in the open for all to see. Which made it all the more troubling for Miriam to understand that in other parts of the country, they were extremely out in the open and quite designed to be seen.

For example, she was aghast to hear from Lila Horowitz at the bakery that a synagogue had recently been bombed in Jacksonville, Florida. Elliot Roth, who worked at his parents' dry cleaning business, added darkly that there had been other such incidents over the past weeks in Miami, Nashville and North Carolina. In those days, not fifteen years after the ovens of the Holocaust were finally extinguished, such news shook the Jews of Paterson in a dimension beyond the ken of a modern reader, charitably removed by time and space from the unspeakable cruelties of the mid-twentieth century.

Word of these troubling events spread through the community in hushed tones between hands of *kalooki*, and in fervent sermons from Rabbi Tishman that the Feldstein family never heard. And as Miriam became more aware of them, she found herself newly cognizant of dots in her life – dots that had never before seemed connected.

With embryonic shame, she realized that she had always looked the other way when spindly Alvin Klein or loudmouthed Herman Gelbart were assaulted by the tough Irish and Polish boys at school, thick lads who were loquacious in a setting where fisticuffs were an acceptable and persuasive extension of language. That Alvin or Herman's fates were a matter of religion would have seemed preposterous to Miriam, so it was never thought of. At least until recently.

Then there was what happened with nursing school. Miriam had looked forward to being a nurse ever since playing doctor as a young girl, and had gotten straight A's since kindergarten. Yet she had been quickly rejected by Seton Hall University, which not only represented a prestigious nursing program, but also a manageable commute. Two of her classmates from Eastside High had been accepted there and neither one was as good a student as she was. Why did that happen? Was it really conceivable that Fiona Morgan and Ann Marie Ruggiero got in because of who they were, and Miriam Feldstein did not because of who she was? In this day and age?

Miriam never thought about the world, and certainly never her own life, in these terms. A strong dose of denial was a key ingredient of the aforementioned psychic insulation, passed on as mother's milk to a people long accustomed to life as the other. But now there were hints and worse than hints of larger, more urgent realities, right here in America, that could not be ignored. Once hearing of them, Miriam found that she could not unhear them.

These previously unconnected dots and others like them flew across Miriam's psyche like a particle storm as Marcel nervously awaited her response in the dark of the car. It was just then that one such dot, previously unnoticed, took root and began to germinate at terrifying speed. What if Marcel's virile otherness was the answer that these questions were plainly calling out for?

Suddenly, miraculously, the dots began to slow. In that moment, she realized that she had intuited the essence of Marcel's confident, soothing lifeforce all along. She'd sensed it the very first time he lowered his voice to her, as he gently guided her courage beyond the beginner slope. It was nothing less than masculine strength personified. It was the sound of safety and protection. And in a moment of blinding clarity, Miriam asked herself what, after all, was wrong with that?

She would never want herself or her child to be a victim of silly, ancient prejudices. My God, you might as well hate someone for being left-handed, she thought. She couldn't bear the thought of tearfully dabbing bloody noses like the ones Alvin and Herman brought home to their grieving mothers, levied without pity on those poor boys for something as stupid and crazy as an imagined deicide thousands of years ago. In this day and age! She couldn't have it.

And looking at Marcel's granite shoulders visibly rippling through his threadworn jacket, she saw she wouldn't have to. Here was a rock of a man from the other side, the dangerous side, one who loved her and could and would protect her, protect her child, their child. A virile, natural, elemental man, a man of the flesh and not the mind, who already loved her enough to renounce everything to be a husband to her and a father to their child. Everything, and now even his faith, he had humbly presented for her dispensation. This monumental offering was proof enough to Miriam of the rightness of their cause and of both their hearts, particularly his.

"You don't need to do that," she whispered to him. "I don't want you to convert."

*

So Miriam never told Adam that his birth father had offered to become a Jew. Years later, she smiled at how callow she'd been on the night she declined his apostasy.

She decided during that wonderful car ride back home that their child would be raised as a beautiful and blessedly secular American hybrid of varied genetic and cultural gifts; aware of, but unburdened by, the weights of religious and class prejudice. He (he!) would be strong and capable and rooted to the physical world, his father would see to that. He would be wise and compassionate and just, raised from birth to be a righteous *zaddik* to everyone, not just the chosen. She would see to that.

Thereby, once past his circumcision (reluctantly agreed to by the father), Adam was always kept at a distance from any ancient dogmas that were meant to spread holiness but so often birthed the opposite. Instead, under the auspices of parents who had determined to live beyond the certainties of their respective faiths, the boy was raised as a sort of new-age *homo Americanus*, tightly wrapped in the insulation of all-men-are-created-equal secular egalitarianism.

In allegiance to this creed, Adam was exemplary. No child in Miss Klein's third-grade class better knew the names of the first Presidents. No fourth grader spoke with as much clarity and passion on the Civil Rights Act, which had just gone into effect, or won as many approving nods from teachers and Black classmates. When the other neighborhood kids sped home from the synagogue to break the holiday fast, Adam had been munching Fritos while watching the World Series, puzzled that Sandy Koufax would not pitch on Yom Kippur.

Part Two

Adam may have been Jewish by the eternal laws of *halakhah*, but in upbringing and in practice, he was the least Jewish boy in the most Jewish neighborhood in town. As he grew older, this paradox gradually became a source of confusion, as did many other facets of his life. Enumerating them would be easiest if begun with his father, who occasionally tried his best, but in the end, proved more of a buddy than a dad.

Certainly, the two of them had some fun together. Marcel

taught his son how to skate in the winter, how to throw a curveball in summer, how to use his fists in all four seasons. Adam's young physique had quickly replicated his father's muscled aspect. Not always knowing his own strength, which was considerable, the boy defended himself from the quotidian menaces of the urban schoolyard with disproportionate verve.

As a result, there were soon few that would cross, much less challenge him in any respect at all. In fact, many of the children began to avoid him out of a vague sense of menace. The Italian boys had tested him, to their misfortune, and it was only the threats of their older siblings that yielded a peaceful modus vivendi. The generally undefeated Black boys carelessly pegged him as another soft Jewish target, but once relieved of this misconception, he was accepted and befriended among them. After a while, all the kids gave Adam a wide berth that precluded any real closeness. Even the teachers seemed to keep their distance.

*

It was decidedly true that Marcel taught his boy to take care of things physically. Unfortunately, these lessons constituted the extent of his fatherly skills. Having grown up as one of thirteen children, he assumed that parenting was a hands-off affair and generally devoid of paternal involvement, apart from any needed discipline. The rest was mother's work, eh?

As a result, evenings that could have been spent with the family were often whiled away at the Question Mark bar, among a crew of fellow expats who dulled their homesick with Ballantine and more. The drinking and absentee fathering did little to endear Marcel to his wife of what had now been ten years. By then, things had been sliding downward for some time, and the end was nearly in sight.

It was hardly surprising then, that when Adam was twelve, his parents called him into the living room for a family talk. Taking a deep breath, Miriam let him know that Mom and Dad were splitting up, but that doesn't mean that Dad doesn't love you.

"He loves you more than anything and that will never change. But Mom and Dad have grown apart, and Dad's family needs him back in Vermont, otherwise the family farm will have to close, and Dad can't let that happen. I must stay here with you, with your school, and also my job at the hospital. So Dad is going back and we'll stay here. But remember, he'll always be your Dad and he loves you and he'll always love you." And so on.

Adam had been girded for this speech. The tenor of their increasingly frequent fights had been obvious enough, and no matter how many times he rooted for Marcel to be a better husband and father, each subsequent shortfall diminished these hopes. For his part, Marcel remained silent throughout Miriam's monologue, and could barely look at the boy before finally calling him over for a deep but finite hug. The next morning, he walked out the door with a single suitcase and returned to the green hills of Vermont.

Father and son saw each other only twice more. At Christmas break, Miriam agreed to put Adam on a train to Burlington, where Marcel picked him up and introduced him to the many aunts, uncles and cousins that he had never met. The boy returned with a lifelong loathing of farm aromas and the burning sense that he'd been made sport of in French. When he turned seventeen and got his driver's license, he drove all day to visit a father who was already shrunken beyond his years, an early and imploding casualty of alcohol, tobacco and despondence. By this time, Marcel had been so distantly removed from Adam's life that his passing from cancer two years later elicited as much rue as mourning.

*

After his father left, Adam's sense of disconnection became acute. He wasn't like the other children, that was obvious, but he didn't know why. They'd stop their laughing and chattering as soon as they saw him, greeting him with cordial friendliness until he moved on, at which point they'd drop their shoulders again. When he waited for the next round of handball during recess, another boy would sometimes step away and give up his turn. In gym class he was unanimously voted the quarterback, the center, the pitcher, the captain. He handily earned the prestigious badge that his mother proudly sewed onto his crisp white gym shorts, proclaiming to the world that her boy had fulfilled the late President Kennedy's Physical Fitness Challenge, during which he had managed an astounding thirty pullups.

Yet every day, the boy came home from school alone. Given Miriam's demanding job at the hospital, he was a latchkey child, quietly watching TV after school, nibbling the fruit and cookies she'd lay out for him each day until she returned from work at six. This might ordinarily be seen as a lot of time alone for a young boy to get in trouble, but Adam never caused trouble. In fact, he seemed to repel it. That is, until one day, when he was on his way to the playground to see if he could scare up someone to play with.

In the distance, he saw that Martin Loewe from up the street was being bullied on all sides by a group of larger boys. Adam wasn't friends with Martin, particularly, nor with anyone else for that matter, but this day, perhaps out of nothing more than boredom, he decided to insert himself into a situation.

He calmly pulled one boy away from Martin and silenced

another with a deep blow to the gut. As two other boys rushed him, he grabbed one by the arm and swung him face-first into the other, knocking both to the ground with shocking force. He wheeled to attack the first two assailants again and quickly punched them to flight. Returning to the boys on the ground, one still in a daze, Adam delivered a beating they wouldn't soon forget, while Martin stood nearby, rubbing his swollen face in stupefaction.

When it was over, Martin couldn't thank him enough, which was the most conversation he had ever offered to Adam, despite the fact that they were the same age in the same school and lived only a block from each other. In his gratitude, Martin invited him to his home for an after-school snack. Adam couldn't remember the last such invitation and accepted it with gratitude of his own. The smaller children on the street, witnesses to this uprising, stared warily at the duo as they ambled off to Martin's house.

"My God, what happened?" asked Mrs. Loewe once she saw Martin's red face and disheveled clothes. "Nothing Ma, it was those jerks again," came the sad reply, "but this time Adam helped me and they ran away."

Mrs. Loewe sized the larger boy up and down. She had noticed him a few times since he and his mother had moved to the neighborhood, and local gossip had it that he was a strange kid, maybe with a disability of some kind. Still, it must be very hard to grow up seemingly without a visible father, not to mention a mother who rarely seemed to be home, shame on her. And he seemed clean and well-behaved.

"Well, I can't thank you enough, young man. That was very gallant of you. Would you like some ice cream with Martin, or would that spoil your dinner?" At the mention of ice cream,

Martin bounded off to wash, while Mrs. Loewe ushered Adam to the kitchen table. "Those older boys, they're nothing but trouble," she groused while scooping out helpings of Sealtest. "They belong in reform school…oh sweetheart, there you are. Bring me two spoons. Adam, do you know my Sarah?"

Sarah was Martin's fraternal twin, but only a purposeful inspection could prove that interesting fact. Whereas Martin still sported his pre-pubescent fragility and a reedy alto that would not serve him well come Bar Mitzvah, Sarah was already well into adolescence, and to Adam, breathtakingly beautiful. How had he not noticed her before? Wait, Mrs. Chapman's class, yes, he'd seen her in the hallway. He never would have guessed she was Martin's sister.

As Adam's eyes met Sarah's they instantly locked and froze and he couldn't turn away. In defiance as much as curiosity, Sarah did not look away either. At which point, their mutual gaze ignited like roman candles into something thrillingly, palpably intense, a deeply visceral sensation far beyond their understandings. It went on long enough to elicit a squint from Mrs. Loewe, which caused both children to turn away with a blush.

From that moment forward, Adam harbored a solemn crush on Sarah. It was more total in nature than a generic schoolboy crush, which can easily change course with a smile or crossed leg. Adam began to think of Sarah as his future mate, the bride of Adam, someone whom he was obviously destined to be with forever. All he had to do was bide his time until they were old enough to consummate what he already saw was meant to be. If there is a God after all, Adam reasoned, he had obviously spoken to them both in that moment. He could feel it, physically feel it. In his mind, he was certain that Sarah must have felt it too, and must have experienced the same divinely ordained glimpse of their electric future together, a future which unfolded and replayed in his mind for many hours and years of his life.

*

Word of Adam's heroics spread quickly through the neighborhood. This resulted in two problems for the young avenging angel. The first was that the boys he'd chased away had brothers and buddies that took issue with his disruption of the natural order. They all came at him, fists at the ready, to restore honor and justice by their squalid terms, and even though Adam gave better than he got with each successive onslaught, it would be weeks before the new natural order was universally accepted.

The second problem was due to the successful outcomes of the first. The Jewish boys of the Eastside – always with greater propensity for the hard sciences over the sweet – now had a formidable protector. Not only was Adam obliged to defend himself from the many predators of the asphalt jungle, it was now his place to defend the other boys like Martin. Nobody asked him to take on this responsibility. It happened organically and he accepted the role gladly, even eagerly, like an understudy whose moment for the spotlight has finally come.

Adam became the defender of the faith, as it were, with a gusto that made him a local legend. When bookish Jeffrey Spiegel broke down and cried that he could no longer endure the torments of the school bus sadists, Adam rectified the situation by slamming their leader's head through the safety window and glaring his posse into submission. When Scott Silverstein was robbed not only of his lunch money, but also the princely three dollars he had saved for a Mother's Day gift, Adam not only retrieved the cash, but also made the offending parties purchase a bouquet for the occasion. Soon, there was nobody left to challenge him, no reason to enforce anything anymore. Adam had brought peace to the land. It was a small miracle.

Around this time, Adam's peers began preparations for their Bar Mitzvah ceremonies. As his own upbringing had been fiercely agnostic, he had been unable to share in their war stories: memorizing four-page haftorah readings versus six, surviving the cigar smoke of the Rabbi's office, managing a pubescent voice that would crack comically and unpredictably. On the one hand, he was certainly glad to avoid all that, but more poignantly, he also felt like he was missing out on something.

This sensation reached its apex when he attended the joint Bar and Bat ceremony for Martin and Sarah. Watching her perform her rites flawlessly, he was overcome with an unfamiliar mix of pride and longing. There she was, his Jewish other half, now a woman, not a girl. It would not be long now. His Bat Mitzvah gift to her was a brooch with a double star of David, which puzzled Sarah before she put it away in her jewelry box, almost to be forgotten.

Adam did not lack for invitations to these ceremonies and the joyful receptions that followed. But the fact that he was never even asked if he wanted his own Bar Mitzvah nagged at his curiosity. Why all the other Jewish kids and not him, he asked his mother? Prepared for this question since before he was born, Miriam was nonetheless caught off guard to finally hear it. She replied a bit too lightly that no religious ceremony would make him any more or less Jewish than he already was, and that he should be happy that he didn't have to go to Hebrew school twice a week – for years! – to prove it.

This was surely not one of Miriam's finest moments, but her perfunctory answer was satisfactory to Adam, though only just. He wanted to belong, and even though he was "just as

Jewish" as any of the boys in the neighborhood, he yearned to be deeper in the club than he felt. One day, alone and bored again, he found himself in a deserted spot along the sludgy banks of the Passaic river. There, he made a small fire – a useful talent learned from his dad – and tempered the blade of his pocketknife until it was nearly red hot. Then he calmly branded a Star of David into his forearm. He never once grimaced in pain.

*

When high school graduation was in sight, many of the neighborhood kids were already deep in their plans for the future. Adam didn't really have a conception of his future, but he knew that more school would not be part of it. He liked the idea of making things, he always had. As a child, he had thrilled to the big machines that hummed day and night in the various factories where his father had worked, staring wide-eyed at the massive, synchronized looms and steaming plastic injection molds.

That these factories limped with much-diminished frequency these days seemed less of a warning to Adam than an opportunity. It simply meant more space and more manpower for his own adventurous ideas of making things – of some kind – when he'd be grown up. As graduation day approached, his life plans had not evolved much beyond this rather vague description.

When class day finally arrived, the kids lined up to have Adam sign their yearbook. He autographed practically every one, as he was quite a popular boy without knowing it. Trailing at the end of the line was Martin Loewe, who after all had played a special role in bringing about his social emergence. Adam had always felt gratitude for this connection and held Martin in a kind of counselor's role regarding neighborhood justice. He inscribed Martin's yearbook and gladly accepted an invitation to his graduation party, to be held that evening at the Loewe's home.

Later that afternoon, Martin read Adam's inscription, which said: "Roses are red. Violets are blue. I am a Jew. Just like you."

*

The party was generally delightful, and it would have been a complete success had it not been a night of tragic downfall for Adam. He may have been a Jew, just like Martin, but his fatal flaw of hubris recalled the ancient Greeks. He arrived at the party in full confidence that childhood was finally over, and that he was finally at step one in his long-awaited plan for a lifetime of making things, with Sarah by his side.

She would complete him at last, become the perfect flowing yin to his granite, steadfast yang. She'd be his loving other half, someday soon the loving Jewish mother to his Jewish children, and the final, perfect cog in his longed-for connection to an identity that had always been just out of his reach; agonizingly visible beyond a transparent rope. In joining with Sarah, he'd finally find a home for his unconnected soul.

In the midst of the party, Sarah's father spotted Adam sitting by himself on the parlor couch. Peering over his orange punch, he contemplated the boy from across the room. This kid from down the street was a strange one, he thought. Always seems so quiet and serious. So stocky for his age, even feels older than the other kids somehow. Driven by curiosity as much as sympathy for a shy boy sitting alone at a party, Mr. Loewe sat down next to Adam and congratulated him on his graduation from high school.

Before the conversation could move much beyond a handshake, he asked the boy what was that on his arm, peeking out from the rolled-up sleeve? Adam proudly displayed the scarred flesh of his home-made Star of David brand, adding with genuine lament that "I was too young to get a tattoo." Mr. Loewe's eyes widened and his stomach recoiled, and suddenly he remembered that this *meshuginah* kid had been *this* close to his daughter – and son! – all these years. Thank God nothing had ever happened. He briskly excused himself to attend to the other guests.

Unaware that his connubial intentions had already been dealt a lethal blow, Adam grew restless and wondered where Sarah was. He found her upstairs with two girlfriends, poking their way through a stack of records. When they saw Adam at the door, the friends got up and told Sarah they'd see her downstairs. They weren't so much avoiding Adam as they were leaving two higher-ups to a private conversation. And, as everyone knew, the rough boy with the big arms should always be given a wide berth.

Sarah had kept a mildly curious eye on Adam over these years. She'd vividly felt the same electricity that he had during that long ago afternoon when they first met. She could even feel it pulsing a little bit just now as he shyly stepped into the room. It was exciting in its strangeness, with obvious energy of some kind that didn't map to any logical or emotional reference point she could think of. She was attracted to him, though she couldn't say how or why. At the same time, she had long understood that at her age, most especially at her age, hormones can and do run wild, without constraints or predictable effects. She had already experienced many similar moments, with many other boys.

But like Adam, she never forgot that first connection, and in this particular moment, she wondered what it was all about. It wasn't a click in the obvious sense. While she didn't yet have a type, neighborhood bruiser was not a likely candidate. There was something foreign about him, ineffable; something wild and unknowable despite his being the boy from down the block. Something hard, with currents of menace, though Adam did not feel threatening. It felt more like having a pit bull in the room; fearsome in capability, but nominally a protective force. Maybe that was it. After all, he'd protected her twin brother Martin, and a lot of the other boys in the neighborhood too, hadn't he? Satisfied with this easy theory, her curiosity quickly faded. She had never felt the need of any such protection herself.

Adam was bashful in getting to the point. "Martin told me that you'll be going to Montclair State. Good to know you'll be around," he said, in a vocal register that surprised them both with its low bass energy. As they smiled at each other with full-on teenaged curiosity, the faint current flowed between them very softly now. In her youth and innocence, Sarah could hardly understand the attraction for what it really was: the residue of something timeless that mattered little to her own time and place, and an answer to fears that were not so much forgotten as unlearned.

She wasn't sure of what to say. Surely she didn't owe him anything – she hardly knew him, really. It was only now that she fully understood that he had feelings for her all along. She said slowly, kindly, as soothing a child, "But I won't be going there, I changed my mind. I'm moving to Israel. I'm going to live on a kibbutz. I decided that I want to live a completely Jewish life."

No one in the house could hear it, but somewhere in the non-material world came the sound of a thousand-pound weight crashing to earth, leaving gravel, pebbles and dust.

*

On a crisp winter's night, some twenty-five years later, Adam and his wife Hyun-Jae held hands as they nestled into a pair of metal folding chairs.

At age twenty three, their son Jason was no longer a child, but they had always enjoyed each of his successes with the same unbridled glee they felt when he'd spoken his first word. There had been many successes since then – spelling and math prizes, a wrestling championship, impressive volunteer work and much more. Young Jason had always made his parents and everyone else supremely proud of whatever he did. He was blessed with the endless talents of his grandmother Miriam, who burst with pride whenever she saw him, and with the magical knack of Hyun's immigrant parents to create contagious warmth and good cheer. Tonight, all of them were delighted to be present at the inaugural graduating class of Jason's first business venture – the Six Points Academy for Taekwondo and Self Defense.

After a brief speech thanking everyone for attending, Jason turned to the fifteen children standing at attention in their *doboks*. He reminded them that their newly acquired knowledge was more than self-defense, and that they had learned more here than mere taekwondo. They had been given a code that they would carry with them for the rest of their lives. To defend not only themselves but others like them who might be in need. To be on the side of right when troubled by the wrong. To be not just strong, but brave and compassionate. "What you have learned here comes from the heart, not just the body," he told them. "And as you leave here today, you all leave as future heroes and protectors, to be loved and respected by future generations to come."

At his signal, the children bowed as one toward Jason. And as he bowed to them in turn, the Star of David that he wore around his neck slipped from under his collar and glinted in the spotlight.

. . .

SINK OR SWIM

Every summer, the tiny, bucolic hamlets of Sullivan County, New York swelled to the brim with endless thousands of Jewish vacationers. The routes of these annual migrations from cities and suburbs were as practiced as any caravan from Gilead or Bukhara. That is, once the travelers recalled the winning answer to the inconstancy of Routes 17 North and South, both of which intersected with a different Route 17 West but not East, with none supplying the necessary Route 17K, which would one day be re-named officially as "The QuickWay," for reasons yet unsolved by any mapmaker or spelling expert.

As the loaded Oldsmobiles and Plymouths traversed these happy courses, children in back seats would gape at the roadside talismans, remembering them exactly from last year and the year before, recalling at a glance which ones meant halfway there and which might yield a needed rest stop. Iconic visuals, such as the massive Ford plant of Mahwah, the Bunyanesque McIntosh of the Red Apple Rest, and the jaunty caricature of Jerry Lewis on the Brown's Hotel billboard, were engraved beyond the science of the finest Kodachromes. Many of these imprints are still not forgotten.

Flowing northward, the highway soon narrowed to a placid quality, befitting its rustic destinations. Here, the cars would slow at each numbered exit, perhaps with a moment's squabble over which one was right and which might be faster, considering all this traffic. Upon leaving the highway, travelers would be greeted at the foot of a curling exit ramp by multiple billboards the size of school buses, each touting the names of dozens of hotels, "resorts" and bungalow colonies, with directions and mileage to each. From a front seat vantage point, these vital instructions were as legible as newspaper classifieds held six feet from the reader's face.

While the drivers lingered to confirm this last leg of the route – no matter how many times they'd read these signs in the past – the cars behind them would often honk their impatience. This naturally resulted in more honking in return, and from other cars as well, sometimes escalating into a sonic facsimile of the city transposed to the country, as if to alert the forests of who was coming. Confused newcomers would hurriedly unfold a cumbersome map from the Esso station, which had promised them a tiger in their tank, though they'd now prefer a compass or divining rod. The honking lasted only briefly, and in truth was probably more expressive of joy than impatience. Everyone had almost arrived.

The air around these villages and townships was impossibly fresh, always overflowing with summer's fecund delights. On a sunny day, one might laze about with a *gluss teh* and watch the ruby-throated hummingbirds joust over fragrant petunias and morning glories. Crab apples would fall from a hundred trees; good for artillery when defending a fort, but too sour for even the most hardened Eastern European palates. Not so for the antlered visitors that were regarded by all as welcome and charming neighbors. When the long days finally seeped into night, the Jews of New York, New Jersey, Connecticut and even Pennsylvania gazed at a vast starscape that was as fine a proof of God's magnificence as any of them would ever tangibly feel on earth. Here the Big Dipper hovered mightily over the entire horizon, emptying its divine sparks into the grateful Little Dipper and the rest of creation; a wondrous tableau broken only by the nervous swoops of brown bats and the distant lamentations of a great horned owl.

For many of these travelers, the allure of the Borscht Belt included proximity to, if not actual residence in, the glitz and prestige of the big hotels, where one might bump into a Hollywood star or even a heavyweight champion. Their names were familiar to everyone: Grossingers, well known as the Waldorf of the Catskills; or The Concord, where one might thrill to Barbra's mezzo-soprano or Woody's standup; or Kutsher's, where your bags might be unloaded by someone not yet called Wilt the Stilt. These palaces and dozens of others less illustrious – The Granit, The Tamarack, The Raleigh, The Flagler and their kind – were the crown jewels of the empire of the Catskills.

Lucky were the boys who got good jobs in these hotels for the summer. Less lucky were the boys who got most of them. Barring the usual acts of nepotism, these important rites of employment, which provided vital funds for college or a car, were attained through a selection process more suited to the Confederate Monticello than the seat of Sullivan County. Upon a cursory registration at "Maury's" employment agency, the hopeful applicant would be told to wait outside, quite literally. There he joined a teeming lineup of other boys on the sidewalk, while overseers from the hotels cruised by, barking out for busboys or bellhops or cleanup crew, choosing the most burly or the most handsome, or by the end of the day, the most determined. Sixty years later, their grandchildren are still picking workers in this time-tested manner, whether Mexican gardeners outside a Miami Home Depot or Russian housemaids off a BQE ramp in Brooklyn.

Luckier still were the girls on these vacations – that is to say, girls past Bat Mitzvah but still unmarried. For many of them, the big hotels were Oz-like destinations for fun and potential romance, and in the days before second cars and easy travel, a valued way to meet Jewish peers from neighborhoods less humble than their own. These young women were frequently advised to keep an eye out for a future dentist or lawyer, and many believed it, for better or worse. Such promising avatars of future security were in ample supply during weekend dances at The Nevele or The Pines, among other hopeful rivals of less obvious gifts. Today, these women and their daughters and granddaughters breathe in a world of panoramic choices, and some might look back with a smile or a shudder at a life strategy so frankly based on hypergamy. But in its day, the wiser heads among the *bubbes* simply called it marrying well.

If the big hotels were the capitals of the Catskills, the bungalow colonies were the quieter surrounding suburbs. Bungalow is a Hindi word for the tiny holiday cottages built by hardy colonials of the British Raj. While no one should fairly compare the accommodations of 1865 vs. 1965, it was only the addition of a refrigerator and stove – and fortunately, but not always, a private bathroom – that marked a full century's progress. An entire family might live for the summer in less than 200 square feet.

One such colony, no different than any other, was called The Five Gables. It was so named for its main building, which fell two gables short of Hawthorne and was painted in a greyish maroon that belied no awareness of any orphans named Anne. It was a generic member of its species, with eight small bungalows set spitting distance from the main house. Each of these diminutive structures sheltered two families that would fill the morning air with the aroma of scrambled eggs fried in schmaltz, accompanied by warm bialys and pletzels lovingly smothered with whipped TempTee. After a leisurely breakfast, the children would scatter – perhaps into the woods – leaving the mothers to kibbitz over their needlepoint in weathered Adirondack chairs plotted in a ring, like a healing circle that would last all summer.

At the rear of the property was an oversized swimming pool that on hot days served as the staging ground for a day's plans, or lack thereof. To most eyes, on most days, this setting presented itself as a nearly unbroken matriarchy. Virtually all of the Five Gables husbands visited only on weekends, and virtually none of the sons of working age would be allowed to loaf around all summer like a *schnorrer*. Left alone during the week with their younger children, the women ruled this refreshing oasis with gusto and fairness. Under their watchful eyes, the smallest kids splashed happily in the shallows, mostly to the annoyance of the older ladies, who like the others, never swam and merely wet their ankles while chanting a liturgical appreciation: *Oy, azoy a mechiah!*

Guarding the pool, and in fact the entire colony, was a singular canine that was a likely admixture of Labrador Retriever and Kodiak bear. Which is to say that the colossal beast named Duffy, held secure by a robust chain, would ordinarily be terrifying if not for his breed's famously amiable temperament. The monster was large enough for the small children to ride like a pony, a pageant he laughingly enjoyed as much as they did. He happily feasted on every fatty bone tossed from afar as the vacationers brought trash past his hut. The imposing sentry barked only in courteous greetings to the residents, preferring stealth over volume while performing any watchful duties. Only once could anyone recall the dog barking in genuine alarm. It was the night that a prowler – or was it a really a bear? – crossed onto the Five Gables periphery. In any case, the intruder was repelled and Duffy soon settled down to sleep, as did the entire colony.

One afternoon the pool had a new visitor, a hulk of a man with a gold tooth and wire-bristle atop a bullet-shaped skull. He was introduced as a cousin, or uncle, or brother, or in law; someone tenuously but veritably connected to somebody else. In these days, barely two decades after the Shoah, blood relatives were in short supply for everyone. Survivors sometimes settled for adoptive relations, and second-generation children were often pleased to discover they had a surprising new cousin. On this sweltering day, the man was deeply content to be here at poolside among these charming ladies of his kith, and supremely relaxed in a chaise lounge with turquoise and orange webbing. He sipped cool seltzer from a Hoffman's bottle, lathered his body with Coppertone, assiduously dabbed zinc onto a granite nose, and gazed out at the woods that reminded him so well of the Bukovina that was once his home.

Most of the children were off playing in these lesser-Bukovina woods. That morning, before the fog of last night's rain had lifted, they had made the intrepid and ritual journey of nearly a quarter of a mile up the road toward Pitkin's Cottages, carrying empty pickle jars and milk cartons. This patrol was on a solemn hunt for the precious rubies of Catskill wildlife, the fluorescent scarlet salamanders that could be seen thirty yards away against the black asphalt, and whose harmless wriggling quickly settled into sullen acquiescence to their unjust confinements. Far from tuckered by these exertions, the boys and even the girls triumphantly brought their amphibian captives straight back to headquarters, where they were joined to the previous week's prisoners, along with any pickerel frogs similarly unfortunate.

One small boy, perhaps four years old or five, sat at the pool's edge, not far from his mother. Perched on an Adirondack, she was scrutinizing her yarn bag for matching colors and smiling with neutrality at the disputes over last night's mahjong. Her child lazily traced a plastic fishing rod in figure eights along the water, first pretending to fish, then pretending to draw, watching the shape of the water magically shift with his speed, force and direction. The unknowable water was endlessly fascinating, trancelike. The chatter around the pool soon decayed into a pleasant lull. The shallow-end splashing of two toddlers melted into peaceful floating on colorful life preservers. In a moment, even the water-painting seemed like overwork for such a beautifully lazy day. Everyone was still and happy.

A shadow rose behind the child, who turned to look up at the imposing figure of the big man, the only man, silhouetted against the August sky. As the boy didn't know him, he felt no apprehension, and as the adults knew that he knew someone else, they felt the same way. Therefore nobody paid much attention when he crouched down and asked, in a key of hurt disappointment, "Why you are not in the water?"

Duffy, chained some ten yards beyond the pool fence,

woofed a tentative bark, and then another. "I don't know how to swim," frowned the boy. "I can only go in the shallow part."

The man peered down at the child, his smile illuminated by a single glinting cuspid. "Of *course* you swim," he confided. "You must know to swim. It is beautiful in the water. And on such a hot day. Water is life. If you don't know to swim, one day maybe you could die."

The boy put down his fishing rod paintbrush and considered this stark viewpoint. Before he could reach a conclusion, he felt himself lifted up to the sky, incredibly high, higher than his father ever lifted him, exhilaratingly high, the best time he'd ever had in his life high. He squealed with limitless delight and grinned wildly above the world in glorious, unfettered joy such as he had never felt. He could almost reach and touch the sun. He was the Icarus of Five Gables, free at last from the tyrannies of earthly reality and all its gravitational encumbrances, seen and unseen. He savored this theophanic ecstasy for nearly three whole seconds before he was heaved like a sack of refuse far into the deep end of the pool.

At once, the boy's entire world collapsed into chaos of the most frightening and intimate character. He couldn't see, he couldn't breathe; he certainly couldn't swim. His doom flashed before him, suffocating him with stinging chlorine in the lungs and eyes. He could only hear things – the percussion of his frantic, hysterical splashing, the kicking and clutching, and the angry barking and snarling of the dog beyond the fence. He struggled to see – why wasn't anyone helping him, why would they let him die? He kicked with all his strength until his head broke above the surface, where he witnessed through tearing eyes the women of the poolside staring in mute apprehension. None of them were going to help him!

The seconds passed like thunder. The child frantically kicked and gasped. Soon seeing that he could grab a breath by bobbing his head above water, he struggled to do it again and again. He despaired to see that he was far – so far – from the yellow rope that marked the deep end. He now recalled that he'd never seen any of these women actually swim, and for all he knew, they were as helpless as he was. Turning in terror from their impassive faces, which were frozen in grainy black and white, he scanned desperately for his mother. She had risen to her feet but stood wide-eyed and terrified behind the outstretched arm of the giant, which kept her distance.

The hound continued its furious barking and gnashing, which echoed from the woods into a cacophony of murderous dogs and the only sounds the boy could hear beyond his desperate splashing. If he could only make it to the shallow end, he could live! He jerked his tiny body toward it and frantically kept bobbing and kicking. It may have taken him an hour or two to finally reach the safety line, or so it felt. But in another twenty seconds, when he was all but certain that his waning breaths were finally spent, and had already come to a possible acceptance of his unfair fate and so made his peace with God, the last atoms of his outstretched fingers touched the weathered cord. In a moment it was in hand, and in a moment more, the sputtering child's feet touched bottom. He was safe at last.

Pulling along the rope, he grappled himself to the pool's edge. Looking up, he saw that no one had moved. All the women were still staring at him. The children in the shallows held their hands to their mouths; one had started to cry.

The man who had inexplicably tossed the boy to his fate stood at the water's edge. His muscular arms, one numbered, were folded in triumph and defiance. His mother's visible terror had simmered into rapid breathing, yet she did not move past the man. None of them moved at all. The boy dragged himself out of the water and coughed out the pool. He glanced up at his tormentor with fear and submission.

The man spoke through an overlord's smile and blustered with sardonic pride, "*Nu, boychik*, you made it, no? Very good! You listen to people like me and you will *survive*. You must always know to survive. Think about it."

With a hatred well beyond his years, one that channeled hatreds he had yet to even learn, with blind hatred that avenged every cowed silence that could never utter its hatred out loud – the child flew into the man with a cyclone of fists and kicks. Bemused, his recipient looked down at the flailing bundle and tried at first to ignore him, then to smile him away. One of the women mutedly tsk-tsked the man; another attempted to calm the boy with compliments on his swimming. The child continued his furious assault until his tiny pounding fists got too close for comfort. The man picked him up again and held him at arm's length. The boy screamed in terror and his mother let out a gasp.

"Bah," he spat with seething disgust. "A *nishtik* herring, *yoh*? He brought the boy's face toward his own and glared directly into the tiny eyes. "You hate me, eh? Even though I help you! You are a little *nar*, a idiot. Still, you will remember one day that I helped you to survive. *Guy avek!*" With that, he tossed the boy unceremoniously into the shallow end of the pool.

There was a burst of silence before the women turned to the man accusingly and began loudly muttering in Yiddish. He looked over each hostile face and attempted to smile their anger away; each attempt failed. Over a mounting din of multicolored accents, a raspy voice hissed a projectile: "*Kapo!*" Another quickly seconded the charge: *"Du bist ein kapo!"* followed by another and a fourth. The word blanched the smile from the man's face, then the color. His mouth curled into grimace. The faces he saw now were pitiless, not friends. He had seen these faces before, frozen in grainy black and white. He wheeled and walked briskly to the pool's exit, slamming the fence shut as he left. The dog continued barking until he was out of eyeshot.

The boy scrambled from the water as soon as the figure was gone. He rushed to his mother and wrapped her legs tightly, strangling his tears like a man. She gently stroked his trembling head. "It's all right, *tateleh.*" In a few moments, the ladies' muttering died down. The birds began to sing again and the endless Catskill summer resumed itself.

• • •

YERIDA

The days go on forever in this crazy place, mused Uri, as he stared out the window into the lethargic June sunset. He wasn't alone in his reverie; at the moment, more than a few of his students were similarly disengaged. It took the abrupt ending of Alex Cohen's stumbling recitation, and the awkward silence that followed, to jolt Uri back to the present. The hot, stuffy, fluorescent, aggravating, dispiriting, endless, ineluctable present.

The silence didn't last, as both nature and nurture abhor these vacuums. For a frightening second, he thought he might have been caught red handed; not even pretending to listen to his own student's recital of a Hebrew lesson that he himself had assigned, and that all twenty of his students were expected to learn, or at least plausibly fake. Instead, the silence was instantly broken by the snap of a rubber band and a yelp of surprise, followed by a loud exhortation to "quit it" and the obligatory laugh track. Scanning his students' faces, he reckoned that only two girls had noticed his daydreaming. One looked away in polite consideration while the other flashed a knowing smile that might have been complicity or something else. These American kids were utterly shameless.

This was only one of the many impressions that Uri Berman had formed in the two years since arriving from Israel with his wife of four years, Chava. The couple had emigrated to teach at the Khesed Academy, the lone remaining yeshiva in Paterson. While the closings of two other such schools in recent memory provided unwanted proof of the city's dwindling Jewish community, those losses were Khesed's gain, so to speak. That said, the windfall in new students, such as it was, posed an ironic but not insignificant problem. Namely, a shortage of local Hebrew speakers who were proficient enough to be teachers, and also hardy enough to teach exceptionally long school days, including after school classes for the Bar-and Bat Mitzvah bound at the nearby Beth Shalom synagogue, and occasional Sunday school classes for the youngsters there as well, and finally, who could work and live and be content with all this on the humble recompense that the academy could still afford.

This last qualification disqualified the qualified that might ordinarily have hailed from not-near-enough Newark or Brooklyn, which the commutes made impossible. Not coincidentally, both places were currently undergoing the same ill effects of the Jewish exodus from city to suburb, and experiencing a similar type of brain drain. The Khesed Academy wrestled with this problem until a helpful friend of the board remembered a nephew that lived in Israel, a good kibbutznik, recently married, who my brother Shmuel says is a talented linguist and bored with collective life and interested in America.

Expensive long distance phone calls made in 1965 shekels and dollars found that Uri and Chava were indeed interested in America, and that Chava already had kindergarten experience to boot. It was a big decision for everyone, and the finance committee had to stretch everything to make it work, but in the end Uri and Chava immigrated to Paterson, into a second-floor apartment in a three-floor building on the mockingly named Park Avenue, just in time for the high holy days. They were given seats for the services at Beth Shalom and introduced to its entire community with tidings of great mutual joy.

That seemed so long ago now, Uri thought, as he lazily assigned the next recitation to Arlene Sussman, who could be counted on as an exemplar of diligent homework. As she read her lesson with flawless diction, Uri felt proud of his teaching for a brief moment, but his mind soon cajoled further wandering. He quickly scanned the faces to confirm his suspicion that no one cared about Arlene's example anyway. Most were looking out the window or at their watch, even as the wall clock loudly and slowly ticked the twelve long minutes remaining until six PM. It was wrong to end class early of course, but everyone wanted it. Succumbing to this unspoken weight, Uri dismissed them as soon as Arlene was finished. All except Marc Weinbaum, who was instructed to stay behind.

When the class had emptied except for Uri and his twelve-year-old captive, he leaned into the boy with a montage of facial and vocal expressions that moved from cold scrutiny to outraged shock, followed by infinite sadness, jeering accusation and stern paternalism. All of this while young Marc looked on in poker face and heard the charges. He had announced to the class last week that he'd raised more than sixteen dollars in *keren ami* charity collections for Israel, on top of another ten claimed the week before, but upon submission, his collection box yielded less than two dollars in coins. Breaking the eighth or ninth commandments are both sinful, Uri gently warned, but being a thief – a *ganav* – was worse than not telling the truth. Now that the class is empty and I've shielded you from public shame, which of these two was the case, son?

The boy didn't quite have the heart to look Uri in the eye, and in turning away it was easier to offhandedly allow that he had done only a little of both. "I really raised only eight dollars, and I only took two."

The audacity of this defense was highlighted by a reminder that there was only one dollar and eighty five cents in the box, and either one can't count or one has made a mistruth even worse. None of this troubled young Marc especially, nor did the promise that Uri would be reporting this incident to the rabbi, and that there will be consequences, and you may go now, good evening.

*

It wasn't a good evening, groused Uri, as he trundled his quarter mile walk to their boxy Eastside abode. Chava would not be home that night until much later. The much-beloved wife of Beth Shalom's cantor had just passed, and the rabbi's wife had asked if Chava could please help out with the shiva, which of course she was happy to do. That meant a cold evening alone for Uri and a wilted salad, perhaps watching one of the three channels their donated Sylvania portable could often receive. Or maybe not, maybe he would read instead. He often said that, though he rarely did so these days. He had so little time for it since moving here and bringing his English up to par. So little that he mostly lost interest in reading for pleasure or knowledge. Which was to say that he had lost a piece of himself.

Uri was already dressed for bed by the time Chava returned. She kissed him on the cheek lightly, mechanically, almost without looking at him. It was a kiss that unwittingly stung. During those lean days following their arrival, when they could barely afford necessities, much less amusements, the couple had introduced a layer of romanticism into their relationship that had never flowered in the old country, and was not always present or even valued in the no-nonsense attitudes of the kibbutz. Bombarded by so many American messages to the effect that "all you need is love," and by endless images, jingles and commercials hawking beauty and sex and personal gratification, the bemused immigrants adopted a when-in-Rome attitude that amounted to both an erotic awakening and a ready source of cheap entertainment.

Though no poems were ever written, it had actually been quite a beautiful time for both of them, and very romantic in its way. Lamentably, those fires had quelled to embers some time ago, until they became rote and more rote until they were just one more rote thing, finally dissolving into this ignominious peck on the cheek that depressed Uri disproportionately. The fact that Chava had blithely gone back to the kitchen without noticing his mood made him feel even worse.

When the couple turned off their bedside lamps after saying their prayers, the silence was palpable. Almost simultaneously they asked if something was wrong, producing smiles in the darkness and a touching of feet under the covers. Uri let her speak first. She was tired after a long day of cranky first graders, followed by a long evening helping with the many mourner guests. Fortunately, she had a very nice supper from the spread at the cantor's house and met some lovely new friends, how about you?

Uri had long stopped boring her and himself by recounting the daily frustrations of his teaching life. Recently, his frustrations had acquired a more ambitious dimension: it was America itself that was frustrating him. So crass. So lacking in seriousness. So grossly consumerist, didn't people see it? Uri had been raised on one of the Marxist-inspired kibbutzim that dotted the early days of the Zionist pioneers. He grew up believing that money and greed were both sides of the same coin and vowed never to be bound by either. But here they were, both of them bound to it all the same, tenuously hanging on in the belly of the capitalistic beast he'd been taught to despise. It was too much to complain about, certainly at bedtime. He shut himself down and simply whispered with an ironic tone: *another day, another dollar.* At this they murmured a pleasantry, turned their backs to each other and waited for sleep.

On his side of the bed, Uri stared into the web of shadows cast by the streetlight. He hadn't said what was on his mind, but the words still buzzed like angry hornets. *He just wasn't sure this situation was working out.* He was bone tired at the end of the day, every day. It wasn't just the long hours. These were compounded by the draining recognition that most of his students didn't care a flying drop about his earnest lexical impartations, no matter how expertly conveyed.

He figured most of them would probably never speak more than a word or two of Hebrew anyway, for the rest of their lives, if at all. Once they've enjoyed their gaudy Bar and Bat Mitzvah parties they'll move on from it, he thought. They'll retain just enough of the mother tongue to check some psychic box and maybe read the Four Questions before passing them on to a sibling. Not that Uri cared so much that his students were quickly and clearly losing their Jewishness, if such a thing were indeed possible. In the mythologies he'd absorbed at kibbutz Beit Achdus, religion vied with capitalism for leadership among the world's most regrettable ills.

So what if he was never much of a believer? So what indeed, but he knew to never ask such questions out loud. If he had, they never, of course, would have been hired to come here. Fortunately, the elders at Khesed had been satisfied enough that this couple checked so many important boxes themselves. As the Academy needed Hebrew and Sunday school teachers far more urgently than religious scholars, adequate observance of the ancient laws was simply assumed of the two Israelis. No, these weren't religious doubts that Uri was feeling. They were doubts of a more pedestrian kind. Doubts about money. Doubts about the future. Doubts about happiness. These were doubts he had never felt before. These were *American* doubts.

On her own side of the bed, Chava was closer to sleep than Uri, but still tingling from her evening. She had known Rifka Krakauer the cantor's wife very well, and would have volunteered to help with the shiva visitors even if she hadn't already been tasked for it. Poor Rifka, thank God it was swift and there was no pain. She was loved by so many, Chava marveled. She had never seen such a cavalcade for one person. While her own kibbutz of Zehuyot was less dogmatic than Uri's, it was still largely insular, not to mention geographically remote. The passings of even the most revered elders gathered only modest gatherings; not like the dozens that had come to the Krakauer home to pay their respects, and this was only the first night! To have touched so many and be loved so broadly by so many people, like a famous person almost. It was a notion that she may have read about or dreamt about when she was a girl.

It was certainly not what she had dreamt of when she met Uri, who had arrived at her kibbutz one day along with a van full of visiting relatives. They noticed each other immediately, he every bit the dashing sabra in his tightly rolled-up sleeves, she with her coal-black hair and cat-almond eyes, both introduced into her bloodline centuries ago in some pitiful corner of the pitiless steppes. Throughout the day's visit, he made her laugh with his clever wordplay and intrigued her with his passion for languages. She beguiled him with the subtlety of her conversation and obvious depth of feelings, along with a smile that evoked everything that was missing from Uri's life. All of these qualities would be appreciated and built upon in the future, but they likely didn't matter as much as the fact that Uri and Chava were both of marrying age and marrying desire, and without attractive matches elsewhere in sight. They liked each other from the start, but had probably decided to get married before the afternoon was out.

That was almost five years and two hemispheres ago, thought Chava. And still no children, still no children. Of course those would be very difficult now, they were barely managing as it was and she had to work, besides. But in two years of trying in the old country there was nothing. Even the lustful days that Uri had prodded for them when they first moved here, when they made love every day, sometimes more than once a day, had brought no sign of a family. That was why they came here in the first place, sighed Chava. If there had been children, they never would have left their homes, their friends, and the tenuous fragments of relatives still scattered about the holy land.

Coming to America seemed a good idea at first and it still seemed a good idea, thought Chava. *It was actually working out.* She delighted in her surrogate children from the K-1 classes, and gave them an indelible love that many would recall for the rest of their lives. She easily made new friends among the synagogue community, and once she got the hang of it, quickly adapted to urban living and the running of a private home, small as it was.

If only Uri were more happy, she thought, although this was not yet a word she felt comfortable using. At least if he were less grumpy and dour, he was never like that before. She had rationalized that it was just an acclimation that was taking longer than hers, a phase he was going through, like those lustful months when she had alternately played the lover, the courtesan, the stranger and even the virgin (again) for his benefit. She still loved Uri and always would. But this man was less Uri by the day, and his dissatisfactions were proving contagious.

*

The next day, Uri received a note from Rabbi Friedlander to meet in his office after school, informing him that the mother of the boy with the missing charity money, the Weinbaum boy, would be coming in to hear his opinion.

"My opinion? He is a spoiled brat with no moral center," thought Uri, smiling at the recently learned adage that honesty is always the best policy. He had hoped this issue had been kicked upstairs to the rabbi, to be dealt with on terms of discipline, not negotiation. He frankly couldn't imagine what his opinion would add. If the boy raised the money and stole some, it was one thing. If he didn't raise the money in the first place, despite lying twice to the class that he had, then it was another. He had already admitted to both these transgressions. This was hardly a case for Talmudic dissection.

When Uri entered the rabbi's office, Mrs. Weinbaum was already seated and glanced up with an icy smile. The rabbi began by asking Uri to repeat the nature of the problem, which was surprising, as Mrs. Weinbaum must already know, or else she wouldn't be here. In his still-imperfect English, Uri tried his best to recount the situation in the most diplomatic way he could, as both listeners stared at him.

When he was done, there was a heavy silence. He looked to the rabbi, who looked to Mrs. Weinbaum who looked back at Uri with an expression poised deftly between relief and annoyance. Looking straight in his eyes, she informed them both that young Marc must have misspoken when he said the wrong amount that he raised. It was really the amount he was *expecting* to raise. Both a neighbor and a relative had promised him donations, but they hadn't made them yet. And if there's *any* shortfall at *all*, she and Mr. Weinbaum would be glad to correct the amount, *whatever* the correct amount is. Another silence followed before the rabbi noted that the boy had no history of trouble and was said to be coming along nicely with his Bar Mitzvah lessons, please remind me of the date again?

Upon reminding him, Mrs. Weinbaum rose to leave, and studiously avoiding Uri's eyes, concluded the meeting by saying "I hope this incident will be of no further trouble to you or my son, rabbi."

Rabbi Friedlander motioned for Uri to stay behind. Once the door was safely closed, he explained that he himself had phoned to speak to the family about the incident and it had already been solved, more or less, but Mrs. Weinbaum wanted to come in and hear it from the horse's mouth, so to speak.

"Did she not believe you, rabbi?" asked Uri.

An uncomfortable moment was spent judging whether this was an impertinence. "The Weinbaums are respected members of our community," Rabbi Friedlander explained. "They are also influential members of the local business community and generous benefactors to the synagogue and its activities. If there was a misunderstanding about the boy's charity collection, or even if something was amiss, it is best dealt with by the family, and I made certain that the family understood our concerns." Seeing that the situation was theoretically solved, Uri asked if there was anything else. The rabbi eyed him quizzically before dismissing him and moving his attention back to his paperwork.

The audacity of it, fumed Uri, as he sidestepped puddles in the blood-orange gloaming. Money really is everything here, just as they sneered back home when he announced his plan to emigrate. Your kid can be a liar and a thief, and the parents won't care a bit, they'll even lie on top of it for good measure. And the rabbi – he spoke as if I were the problem! Well, maybe I am, Uri thought. Maybe go-along-to-get-along really is the way things work here, even though this was an adage he had yet to hear in English. It was as if he was the schoolboy to sit shame faced in front of the rabbi! What is this place? This elemental question started bouncing in his mind like one of those pink rubber balls the kids were always bringing to class. What is this infernal place and why am I here?

Such questions are timeless to immigrants the world over who find themselves lost or foundering. As if on cue, one of their timeless answers appeared in Uri's path. To his left was a glowing neon sign of welcome in the window of Duggan's Tavern, a local bar that he passed every day without notice. He slowed his pace and considered a drink. He didn't usually drink. At home there was the obligatory and largely untouched amphora of chocolate-orange Sabra liqueur. It was a product he came to loathe as much for its taste as his knowledge that it came from the head *ganav* of Seagram, heir to a bootlegger's fortune.

As he slowed his step, the idea of something that could numb his anger seemed eminently reasonable. Another man passed him into the tavern, and before the door could close, Uri found himself inside. The bartender, a barrel-shaped man with an ill-fitting vest, glanced lazily at the unfamiliar face and went back to wiping mugs. Three barflies didn't look up from their glasses, while a fourth hunched over the prismatic hues of a Wurlitzer juke box. Uri stood frozen. He sensed he shouldn't be here. He sensed he was out of place. He sensed coarseness and loneliness and even a hint of violence. When someone asked loudly if he was going to shut the fucking door buddy, you're letting the cold air out, he turned on his heels and briskly continued home to his dark and once again lonely apartment.

*

Tonight, not even a wilted salad was waiting. With Chava so busy with classes and the Krakauer shiva– how many more nights would it be again? – no one had bought groceries and his lunch had been crackers and a sliced tomato. It was too late to shop and cook, and Uri was famished. While he'd have to justify the cost to Chava, he put on his coat and walked a dozen blocks to the Moonbeam Deli, one of the last kosher (style!) restaurants left in the city.

The overwarm place was nearly empty, save for the room-filling aroma of countless fatty sandwiches gone by. A Puerto Rican teenager was gingerly cleaning out the slicer, while an older man sat alone in a corner of the dining room, drinking tea and reading *The Forward*. Looking up, it took him a moment to realize that he had a customer. He motioned for Uri to sit anywhere he liked.

By now Uri's hunger had overtaken his anger, and he was neither surprised nor ungrateful when the man approached him with a menu, explaining that the waitress was off that night. He ordered a vegetable cutlet – how he missed the falafel from home – figuring this was the closest he was going to get to a non-*traif* meal in a "kosher style" restaurant. He didn't know what the phrase kosher style actually meant, so when the other patron, who was also the host, the waiter and now also the bus boy, came to set his table, Uri smilingly asked the question out loud.

"I can hear that you're a sabra," grinned the older man. "*Bagrisn, boychik*, welcome! *Du redst Yiddish*? "Not very well, I am afraid," replied Uri.

Undeterred, his host took a seat and introduced himself as Morris Blumenstyk, the owner of this establishment. "We've been here for thirty-five years. My brother, may he rest in peace, and I opened this place in 1932. Back then this was a very *haimische* neighborhood, we used to have lines out the door! On weekends we couldn't even keep up with the crowds. We would sell out of corned beef, would you believe it? Nowadays we're mostly dead, as you can see. Our kind, they're all leaving, *gay gezunterheit*. So what brings you here?"

Uri was in a serious mood and ready to consider this question's metaphysical dimensions, but the man's affability was infectious. "Mostly an empty stomach," he smiled, "And to know what 'kosher style' means in practice." "Ah, I see you have the Jewish gift for comedy," Morris winked. "Tell me, what brings a funny sabra like you to Paterson, New Jersey? All the Jews are leaving, so you decided to come?"

It was not something that anyone expected, but somehow over the next hour, Uri poured his heart out to his host. He began slowly and carefully, making certain to say respectful things about everyone and everything that comprised his American life so far. But this cautious trickle soon grew into a running stream of pointed observations and unsettling questions, and by the second cup of tea, a veritable river of well-elucidated frustrations. Mr. Blumenstyk absorbed all this in patient silence, nodding sympathetically during the scattered breaks of the diatribe. When it was over, Uri looked up at his host with the cheerless eyes of a man who has just narrated his own defeat. Regaining himself, he apologized for his "outburst" and making a motion for his coat, asked for a check.

"Look, sit, never mind the check. Dinner is on me tonight, how about that?" offered his host. "Alvaro, let's close up, ok? Nobody's coming."

The young man had finished cleaning and wrapping and had been silently watching the Yankees-Senators game on a battered Philco behind the counter. Wishing him *buenas noches* and receiving a *goot nokt* in return, Morris locked the door and turned off most of the lights. In the semi-darkness, the dining room looked mysterious and slightly clandestine, with only a dim spotlight pointed at the host's back table. Morris poured fresh water for the tea and patted his hand on Uri's shoulder in sympathy before re-taking his seat. At that moment, Uri couldn't remember the last time someone besides his wife had touched him.

Morris slowly stirred his tea, which he took from a glass, and cleared his throat before meeting Uri's dejected eyes across the table. "I hear what you're saying loud and clear," he pronounced. "You shouldn't be ashamed of these feelings. It's different here, just very different. You just have to understand better where you are. America is one big melting pot, they say. But what they *don't* say is that it's the fire what's *under* the pot that's really the point. Black, white, Jewish, not-Jewish, Puerto Rican, whoever. The fire that melts the melting pot is business, it's money. Without money there is no life here."

This note cut through Uri like a hot blade as Morris continued. "You came here thinking that you and your wife could have a nice quiet sabra life here in *America*" – this he pronounced with a pointedly comical accent – "but then you find out that teaching Hebrew to *Americanishe* kids who don't want to learn isn't a business. It's more like *tzedakah*, like charity work. *Farshteist*? You understand?" Uri looked up at him with a mix of shame and curiosity. Morris completed his endless stirring and took a sip of his tea, sighing with pleasure at its perfect temperature.

"This country, *keneine hora*, is precisely the opposite of the one you came from. You came from a place where people *return*. They arrive from all over the world to *correct* the past. Your own parents were maybe among them. This place is exactly the opposite, *pinkt fakert*! People come to this country to *leave* the past. Look at the big shots, the *groisse machers*! Who was Andrew Carnegie? A *shmeggege*, a nobody; a bobbin boy who worked in the textile mills, just like the ones here in town. Now you can't go hear Beethoven without seeing that *goniff's* name at the top of the program. Who was Levi Strauss? *Achh*, a peddler! Now you see his name on every second *tuchus*, everywhere, I swear. *Nu*? You think Levi Strauss sailed across the ocean so he could be a more well-off Bavarian?"

Uri heard all this with astonishment. He hadn't expected this outing, this meal or a meeting of any kind. He didn't expect to pour his troubles out to a stranger. He certainly did not expect that a delicatessen owner should harbor such curiously incisive perspectives. He had clearly underestimated the man, and in that moment understood it was far from a first offence.

"You have been very kind," he said, reaching for his coat in earnest now. "I appreciate your generosity for listening to me. I have kept you late, I am afraid. I will pay you for the dinner, please."

Morris let out a chuckle. "I see, Mr. Funny Sabra, that you didn't hear me so well. Or maybe you did hear me and you didn't understand. Or maybe I'm just a *meshugginah* old man who talks too much, yes? But maybe you'll think a little bit about what I just said to you. You can devote maybe a drop of that *yiddishe seichel* to something you've heard here tonight. And don't worry about the check, I said it's my treat and my pleasure. Here, learn something new and useful from the Americans: Don't look a gift horse in the mouth."

As they walked to the door, Uri didn't know what else to say to this kind man. His mind was spinning on arrival and now rotating on another axis. At a loss for more genuine words, he wheeled and said, "You never explained to me what "kosher style" means?" Morris laughed that this was a complicated question for another night, and that he looked forward to that soon.

"Then answer me one more question," asked Uri, as he warmly shook the extended hand. "How is it that you speak so much Yiddish even now? Surely few others do?"

"Me, I love languages, I do," Morris beamed. "It's a hobby of mine. I even read *The Forward* in Yiddish too, maybe you noticed?" Not waiting for an answer, he continued, "My whole family spoke it at home, that's all we spoke together. My father came here across the ocean too. He was a weaver from Lodz, back in the old country. I mean, *our* old country. Our people found good work here in the mills. My father was also a labor organizer. He was a part of the great Paterson Silk Strike for worker's rights, it was a famous thing, back in 1913, you should look it up. I would have been there myself, but back then I was just a *pisher.* Nu? A good enough story? We'll talk more next time. *Zei gezunt!*

As he walked home through the wet, deserted streets, Uri wondered how he would relate this evening to Chava. She would certainly think it unwise and frankly unlike him to be blurting out personal things to who knows who, that might say who knows what to who knows whom in this still-unfamiliar city. He decided that he wouldn't tell her the whole story, just the bones of it. He needed food, so he had a nice meal at that deli they sometimes pass. He'd met the owner, a nice man, end of story. Normally Uri never hid anything from Chava. Complete honesty had always been the golden spike of their union, but in this instance, Uri decided that less was more. This was another Americanism he had recently learned.

When he entered the apartment, the lights were out and he thought Chava might already be in bed, but in fact she had not gotten home yet. At that moment, she was sharing tea with Dr. Sol Levinson and his wife Eva, with their sons Ira and Jonah at The Lampfire, a dark, quiet eatery much favored by Paterson's politicos and community leaders, both above and below board.

The Levinsons were esteemed members of the Beth Shalom synagogue; Sol was a past president and Eva was presently treasurer. The boys had come all the way from New Haven to pay their respects; Yale law and medicine were both in attendance. The family had helped Chava clean up after the visitors and offered her a ride home. As she nestled into the sumptuous leather of Sol's boat-like Buick Electra, the boys announced they were hungry and an invitation was put forward. Now she was sipping something called Darjeeling in a secluded banquette with the Levinsons.

Sol had gently warned Chava that The Lampfire wasn't strictly kosher, but they had a "kosher style" deli menu that the boys always loved; he hoped she wasn't offended by them coming here. "We do our best to keep a kosher home, but we're both so busy that we occasionally find ourselves in a restaurant," smiled Eva "We've been coming here forever," added Ira. "Ever since Jonah's first recital, remember?" Sarah shushed him with a wave of the hand. Chava was encouraged to try the kugel, and although she was curious, she settled instead on a fruit plate that included papaya, which she tasted for the very first time.

They had a lovely repast. Chava couldn't remember the last time she was in a restaurant. She effortlessly charmed the boys and made Eva wish almost out loud that they might meet someone as sweet and serious, sooner than later, God willing! Sol made easy work of his pastrami sandwich, heedless of his wife's counsel that it was late in the evening for such high stakes *fressing*. The most remarkable moment came when Eva asked Chava what she liked most about her life here in America, "Now that you've been here long enough to know."

Clearing her throat and enjoying the strangeness of being the center of attention among grown-ups, she said, "I think what I like best, or at least what I find most interesting, is the mix of different people here, and how they all find a way to live together in peace."

Pressed to expand on this, Chava replied that a simple trip to the laundromat might bring her in contact with more ethnicities than she had seen perhaps in the entirety of her old life. "It is quite an accomplishment, what America has done, an inspiration, really," she marveled. "Who would think that it should work? I would love to see somehow that the secret to this could be used elsewhere in the world, where different people don't get along so well."

Sol and Eva eyed a telepathic exchange. There was a momentary silence before Jonah raised his Coke in a toast: "Wow. What a beautiful thing to say. And I couldn't agree with you more. This city…this whole country…okay, we're not perfect by any means. But y'know what? You're absolutely right. We *are* an example. Of something that's truly special, so special it's never been done anywhere else. And you know what else? *You* are special too. Because *you see it*, not everyone does. You see the greatness of the American experiment and appreciate what it means. For everyone, for the future of everyone."

He raised a glass. "So here's to Chava; here's to the peacemakers!" The family raised their glasses and cups and clinked "To Chava and the peacemakers, *l'chaim!*"

*

The next day, Uri and Chava were awakened by a phone call from the rabbi bearing awful news: Israel was at war with a coalition of hostile states that had vowed its destruction. Classes would not be held that day, and everyone would be advised – implored – to pray for our brave soldiers and for God's mercy once again. The news knocked the wind out of both of them. They had served their time in the Defense Force and knew that many of their loved ones were now in serious danger. They spent most of the day in stunned silence, broken only by prayers and repetitive updates on the radio.

Toward the end of the day, Chava dressed for another night of helping with shiva guests. She invited Uri to join her and pay his respects, which he hadn't done yet, and while it wasn't in his heart to be with other people tonight, he agreed to come. They walked together to the cantor's house. Once there, he said all the right things, exchanged stricken looks with the others and then quietly left to go home.

Despite the five thousand miles that separated him from the battlefields, Uri's anguish and guilt felt as close to him as a migraine. He should have been there; *he just should have been there*. He couldn't go there now though, he couldn't be in Israel in her time of need, not even in an unexpected blast of patriotic fervor. What would Chava do here without him, after all? Would she come with him? How could he afford to go back even if he wanted to, and when would he return "home"?

These were excellent questions, though largely immaterial, as none of them broke the whirring screech of the infinite loop in his head: *I should have been there, I should have been there.* Growing up, Uri and everyone else at Beit Achdus had been intensely aware that while the adults were busy tilling the soil in the Middle East, their families were being rounded up and murdered in Europe. Survivor guilt was branded on him like original sin, as it was for so many others like him who were nearer or further, in space or time, from the literal scenes of the crimes. Now another survivor guilt, in a more acute register, had been levied on him, one he might never live down. As all these thoughts collided, the overlapping layers of pain became excruciating. He never felt so miserable in his life.

He thought once again about a drink and indeed, he'd be passing by Duggan's Tavern in only a few blocks. That wouldn't do, he scowled. He didn't want to talk to anyone, certainly not strangers, certainly not *goyim*, who he wasn't even sure would be sympathetic. He wanted to be alone, but he also wanted a drink, maybe more than one. So Uri continued on past his home, further down toward Broadway, until he stopped outside the dingy lights of Augie's Broadway Fine Wines and Spirits. As he caught his breath and his composure, his eyes lingered for a moment on the pneumatic bikini girls splayed across the Schlitz and Rheingold posters in the window. Outraged by this brief moment of respite, his churning mind roared at him again and angrily reminded him of why he was here in the first place. He firmly opened the door and firmly closed it behind him. The man behind the counter looked up just long enough to squint that he'd be watching.

Uri slowly scanned the shelves with widening eyes – this was remarkable! How much liquor do these people drink after all? There must be hundreds of different bottles. What should he buy to dull his pain? He had never bought liquor before. Gin? No, that was British, he was raised to despise the imperialists. Vodka? Never, nothing from Russia, *puuii*. Whiskey, isn't that what the Americans drink? But which one? Which one would do the job fastest and best? He actually went so far as to ask this question to the man behind the counter. He left with a flask of Old Tennessee and marveled that anyone in this crazy country could spell.

It was an indescribably tense week that followed. Classes resumed with a muted, heavy air as the Jews of Paterson and everywhere else prayed for deliverance. And incredibly, perhaps even miraculously, it came. In less than a week, Israel had won a remarkable victory. The world gasped in amazement. The Jews of Paterson and everywhere else didn't dare breathe relief until deep into the reporting. When the news hit the front pages, there was a joyousness that hadn't been felt in their bones for two thousand years. Uri and Chava were elated; they had witnessed a miracle. They hugged and laughed and made love for the first time in weeks. These were among the happiest few days that either would ever experience. Both remembered them forever in just this way, like a photograph that only barely yellowed.

The high spirits continued for nearly another week, until one day Uri found a note on his desk to see Rabbi Friedlander after classes. Teaching had become somewhat easier, or at least less Sisyphean, these days. The children were in a happy mood, giddy that Israel had survived, swaggering even, as if the outcome had been a matter of common sense. None of these kids, so removed from the events (and so spoiled, he thought), could ever know how narrowly an unimaginable catastrophe had been averted. But there were smiles now, at least. Even Uri managed a smile at a wisecrack from one of the students about Nasser the *plotzer.*

When Uri stepped into the office, Rabbi Friedlander asked him to close the door and have a seat. With a litigious face, he began with a simple question. "Uri, are you happy here?"

Uri had never held an employed position before this present one. At Beit Achdus he had been an equal member of the collective. There was no boss, no employment contract, no hierarchy, no calls for performative deference. Which is why he took the rabbi's question to mean something that it didn't, and answered that "America is still an adjustment, but I believe I come to know it better day by day. *Baruch Hashem.*"

The rabbi wondered if this oblique answer was entirely innocent before continuing. "Today I received two phone calls from our community members; you were the subject of both. I wanted to speak with you privately. I must confess that the calls were distressing." Uri leaned forward in his chair, more curious than concerned. He couldn't imagine what this was about. Smiling as if he were about to hear a good joke, he said, "Tell me, I am intrigued."

It so happened that Uri had been seen coming out of a tavern, one quite notorious in the neighborhood for rough customers and loud bar fights and who knows what criminalities inside. To make matters worse, he was at another time seen loitering in front of a liquor store on Broadway, ogling the pictures of the *zonot* in the window, and furtively slipping a bottle of something into his coat upon leaving.

"I wouldn't have believed these stories had they not come from two separate sources," intoned the rabbi. "Obviously this reflects very badly on everyone if it's true. Do you deny that these things happened?"

Uri was frozen in solid wordlessness. He couldn't lie his way through it, knew he could never pull it off, even if it were the right thing to do, which it wasn't. On the other hand, there were mitigating circumstances that awful night – who wouldn't have wanted a drink? With increasing dismay, he better understood the rabbi's original question.

Opting for an ethical stance and applying the recently learned slogan that the truth is the best lie, Uri replied, "Rabbi, I can only be completely honest. I did not go drink in the tavern. I will say that I almost did; I did step into that place, but for only a moment. I took one look and I left. It was wrong of me to even go that far, I will say, to my embarrassment. But I am not a drinker. And that night that I was at that liquor store, that was the first night of the war. I confess that I didn't know where I was. My closest friends were in terrible danger. Chava, my strength, was not with me in that moment of my weakness, may Hashem forgive me."

"The Lord forgives the righteous," spoke the rabbi, offering only vicarious sympathy. "That said, his children are sometimes slower to forgive. I am sorry to say that we have a real problem here." Uri's outburst of bare honesty lay in melted puddles on the floor.

Rabbi Friedlander continued that "The news of these unfortunate escapades (*escapades*!) has complicated another issue of which we have already spoken once." Uri's eyes widened. Mrs. Weinbaum, the mother of the boy with the mistaken (*mistaken*!) collection box had called again. Apparently her boy was not the only student with the discrepancy (*discrepancy*!) in the collected amount. Another boy was guilty of a similar mistake (*mistake*!) and confessed the deed to his friends, two of whom then gossiped the news to their parents, one of whom called Mrs. Weinbaum, who then wanted to know why her boy was being singled out for shame and discipline by his unfair teacher. In fact, the same parent who called Mrs. Weinbaum was the one that happened to see her boy's Hebrew teacher lurking (*lurking*!) outside the liquor store.

The news is probably all over by now, the rabbi mused. "The community may believe that one of its most important figures is engaged in behaviors that we cannot accept."

Uri the linguist noticed the subtle shift in subject nouns and asked simply, "Is this their view or yours, rabbi?"

*

When the meeting was over and he was slowly making his way home, Uri greedily sucked in the sweet air of Paterson's late spring blossoms. Dogwood, maple, birch, oak, magnolia – one beautiful blooming tree after the other, on the lawns, on the curbs; so many that nobody here even pays attention, he marveled. For Uri, as for so many other Israelis of his generation, planting trees was a sacred act, as close as any secular act might ever come to genuine holiness. And here they're taken for granted like everything else. Kids carve their initials on them and even swastikas, but nobody says or does a thing. What is one to make of such a culture?

This interesting question popped like a soap bubble in light of the larger question of what he was going to do, now that he had been suspended from teaching. It should not be called a suspension, said Rabbi Friedlander, who framed it as more of a sabbatical. "It would be good to create some temporary space from this situation, and some space for you."

Uri didn't blink when he heard what would happen. He had recently learned the adage that discretion was the better part of valor, and unaware that Shakespeare was his co-pilot, he remained silent during the rabbi's described remedies. Besides, he had already spoken the truth and it had come to nothing. What more could he say, other than yes, a sabbatical would make the most sense for everyone?

With a small smile from the rabbi and a larger smile from Uri, it was learned that through the generosity of the Khesed Academy's board of directors, of which Rabbi Friedlander was a member, Uri would be kept on salary for the sixty days that had been prescribed for his exile. "Please understand this as an act of utmost faith on our part," said the rabbi firmly.

When he saw Uri's still-fearful expression, the rabbi shifted into a more empathetic tone. "I can understand how you must have felt that terrible day," he murmured sadly. "You were under a great deal of emotion, as we all were. In a moment when you should have turned to prayer, you yielded to a temptation. They are, unfortunately, all around us here. But perhaps just as importantly, you see now that impressions matter. Oh, maybe too much, but people believe what they see. Our sages teach us to see more deeply than the eye can take in; to look more deeply, in order to find truth. We, and I, believe that there is a larger truth to you than these incidents would imply. We would ask you to use your time away wisely, to seek your answers within

God and the Torah, and be prepared to rejoin us in the fall with a fresh approach."

When Uri arrived home, Chava was already seated at the small Formica table where the two took their spartan meals. She was facing away, toward the miniature window that had been squeezed into the miniature kitchen to accept only the minimum possible slants of fresh air and sunlight. Removing his jacket and shoes but still not hearing a greeting, he approached to find that she had been crying.

"What is it, Chava, what has happened?" "Don't you know already?" she asked angrily. "A *shikkor*. In my house. My husband. A lush!"

Uri stepped back and affecting a brave face said, "I don't know what you're talking about. If this is about some gossip that has been going around, I can assure you that gossip is very cheap and usually untrue." Another expression he had recently heard was that if one couldn't successfully dazzle with brilliance, one might alternatively baffle through a strategic application of bovine spoors.

Chava was not to be placated with such leavings and angrily began to well up again. "I smelled it on you the other night. I didn't believe it; I didn't want to ask about it. I pretended it didn't happen, I thought it must be in my mind. Then the next day I found your bottle when I was cleaning. Almost empty! Hiding it in the house! This is what sick people do, Uri, here they call them alcoholics. And now everyone has seen you! Mrs. Shulman in the office told me about it, told me she was sorry to hear such news. I was so embarrassed. I didn't know what she was talking about, and then all at once it made sense – the smell, the bottle, the way you've been for so long now…it all made sense." At this, Chava stopped fighting her tears.

Uri had already been prepared for these tears on account of his suspension, or rather, sabbatical. But he was not prepared for news of his scandal – goodness, they call this a scandal? – to have landed with his wife before he could attempt to explain himself. He tried telling Chava his side of the story, and though he did earn a touch of sympathy, his full explication did little to lighten her mood. She barely reacted when Uri said that he'd still be getting his regular paycheck during this…sabbatical. In fact, she didn't say a word before looking deeply into his eyes and asking bluntly, "Uri, are you happy here?"

*

They had never had such a conversation. They never once talked about being happy because it never struck them as a legitimate topic. They had always assumed that happiness was simply freedom from unhappiness. They'd both grown up in the knowledge that they were building a new Jewish nation, literally, and in doing so, helping to right tremendous cosmic wrongs; a serious business if ever there was one. In light of such a weighty mission, asking for more than the elemental satisfactions out of life seemed decadent, if not childish. The idea of shaping one's life to pursue such a nebulous concept – after all, what was happiness, anyway? – was the kind of self-centered things the narcissistic Americans did. But now they were Americans too, weren't they?

In due course, Uri discovered that a more important issue had prompted his wife's frank question. As it turned out, the Levinsons, whom Chava had spent such a lovely evening with at The Lampfire, called a few days later with an interesting proposal.

"Mrs. Levinson was a close friend of poor Rifka, and Dr. Levinson is a personal friend of Mr. Abraham Ovitz of New

York, who you probably know is a wealthy philanthropist for Jewish causes. You sometimes see him in the newspapers," she explained. "Mr. Ovitz is beginning a new charitable organization called Shalom Gadol, which will support peace projects all across the world – anywhere Jews live. It is a very worthy mission, very important work, especially now. He has been looking for an assistant to work closely with him, someone bilingual, and the Levinsons recommended me." Uri took all this in with some incredulity, but as Chava went on, an unnamable feeling crept through him, something distantly related to relief.

"I had a long telephone call with Mr. Ovitz yesterday," she continued, "and while of course he will need to meet me in person, I have a strong feeling that he will want me for this assistant position. Sarah Levinson told me – how do they say it here? *It's in the bag.* The major issue for us to consider – for you to consider, dear – is that if I were to accept, it would mean a lot of travel for me. Many days of travel at a time. We would not have as much time together, not nearly. Which is why I ask: Uri, are you happy here? I am no longer certain that I am."

Thus began the deepest conversation they'd ever had together. Neither had ever talked about any personal goals, other than to be loving parents, which had never happened, and faithful Jews, which they already were, more or less. Uri had little new or surprising in answer to whether he was happy; his moods had been eloquent enough. Chava was the only one in the world who understood him, and knew well that he was a fish out of water, as they said here. He poured his heart out to her and welled up more than once. When she stroked his cheek to soothe him, he felt a gentle warmth that he began to understand as a microscopic particle of happiness.

For her part, Chava had been nervous that Uri would immediately reject any notion of her leaving the kindergarten in order to advance world peace. He would, after all, be alone much of the time without her, and who would want that? Even though she would earn more money, and they might actually be able to create some savings, what would be the purpose? To buy a house where they wouldn't live together very often?

As Chava described her opportunity and its particulars to Uri, her initial feelings of flattered surprise began to give way to an escalating confidence and exhilaration that grew with each new sentence. By the time she was done speaking, she had visualized something that she'd never seen before. She pictured herself as a someone. A someone who was something more than just anyone. Someone not just passively living in the world as it is, but someone with the privilege to shape the world, help change it, in substantial ways, active ways, not just quotidian acts of *tikkun olam*.

It was an intoxicating notion. She could apply her people skills to other adults who were also somebodies, who in their own ways were also shaping the world. She could apply her organizational talents to meaningful diplomatic and charitable events, instead of alphabetized coat pegs. Not least, she would have a chance to see the world – all those capitals that Mr. Ovitz had mentioned! – and she'd see Israel again. It would be so good to be with everyone again.

Uri and Chava talked deep into the night and both were exhausted by the time they got to bed. They both believed, with much truth, that tonight they had shared themselves naked in a previously uncharted way. Once in bed, they embraced each other tightly, for a long time, even dozing off intertwined, as they once did under the shade of olive trees. When Uri awoke, he was alone and startled; Chava was gone and he would be late for work. It took him a moment to remember that he had no work. Nothing other than the job of figuring out what he was going to do with himself for the rest of the day for the next two months, and after that, for the rest of his life.

She left a note to say she would be back in time to make dinner. Until then, Uri was alone, with nothing to do. He looked at the apartment with a low-grade nausea. They had never really made it their home, it had always felt temporary. They had never bothered to find two more chairs for the table, as the squat linoleum kitchen was too small for guests in any case. He peered at the measly few books he'd been able to acquire at rummage sales and library discards. His own shelves mocked him.

Sipping his morning tea, he felt happy for Chava, really. If she ended up with this position he would miss her very much, he loved her after all. He had always been a good husband to her; kind, thoughtful, strong, and sober, notwithstanding the mistaken gossip of housewives. But this was no life for her, or for him, or them. Together in America, they had gamely run a treadmill that would always leave them in the same place at best, fueled by a joint agreement of narrow expectations they had expected to last forever. Unfortunately, it hadn't.

Uri decided to take a long walk. As if to avoid more trouble, he chose a direction opposite Duggan's Tavern. This strategy served little benefit, as it wasn't many minutes before he passed at least half a dozen similar establishments. It was true that Uri "wasn't a drinker" and he reasoned that the only thing that had steered him that night to Augie's Broadway Fine Wines and Spirits was his anguish over the war. This association validated his previously held view that alcohol is simply a remedy for pain. Looking out at so many bars and taverns, he was aghast at how much pain there must be here in Paterson. At least he was not alone.

He wandered for hours. He lingered through the magnificent Eastside Park, where he observed statues dedicated to Civil War heroes. He was moderately aware that the Americans had fought a bloody Civil War in their history, but knew little about it. Did the Americans really sacrifice half a million people to free their own slaves? It was incredible. If Pharaoh and the Egyptians had been as evolved as Lincoln and the Americans, who would Moses have been and who would we Jews even be today?

Strolling further, he came across a statue dedicated to Kazmirez Pulaski, a Pole who had apparently been an important general in the fight to create America. A Pole, of all people! Many of the founders and families of Beit Achdus could trace their roots to Poland, more or less. None had anything good to say of their former neighbors, to say the least. Yet here one of them – a Count, no less – had given his life to the idea that all men are created equal. "I must be missing something," mused Uri. "There must be more to this."

*

By the time he was hungry for lunch, Uri had worked out an idea and headed straight to the only friend he thought he could tell it to. The lunchtime crowd, such as it was, had mostly died down at the Moonbeam Deli, leaving only a few seniors still nursing their morning teapots and kibbitzing over melba toast. In his regal corner sat Morris Blumenstyk, who smiled broadly at Uri and motioned to come join him. In seconds, a waitress brought a fresh pot of tea and a cup for Uri, and placed bowls of half-sour pickles and saltines.

"I wouldn't expect to see you here at lunchtime, Mr. Funny Sabra. Shouldn't you be punching the clock *mit de yeshive bucharim*?" "English, please, Mr. Morris," smiled Uri, "Or at least Hebrew. This is an *effscher terrier* of a language you are speaking to me."

Morris eyed him suspiciously. "I thought you don't speak Yiddish, you told me. What do you mean, *effscher*? That word means *maybe*. Are you sure you aren't using the wrong word? " Yes, *effscher* does mean maybe," Uri grinned. "And terrier, this is a dog, a *kelev*. The expression was told to me by one of the students who proudly talked about his dog. His parents assured him that it was an exotic pure breed, a 100% *effscher* terrier. Maybe this, maybe that. The boy didn't know it was a mutt."

Morris broke out in loud peals of laughter and soon Uri joined him. "That's a good one, Mister Funny Sabra, an excellent jest! Next you'll be at Grossinger's with Buddy Hackett, signing autographs. *Effscher* terrier! I must remember that!"

Uri wound down his own laughter; he realized that he hadn't laughed in a long time. He took a sip from his cup and realized it was tea when he really wanted coffee. By the time the waitress took his order, he changed it to a Coke. He leaned in and asked, "And that is what America is, is it not? A maybe-this-maybe-that mixture of everyone in the world. And maybe – *effscher* – just as the mixed breed is usually the healthiest and strongest, maybe this place is creating something astonishing." Morris raised his eyebrows and stirred his tea. "*Nu?* So what brings Mr. Funny Philosopher to the best kosher style deli in these parts, at this hour of the day?"

Uri told Morris his grand idea, which was to spend his sixty days of "sabbatical" seeing the country. "I will never have another chance like this," he confided. In two months he could go coast to coast on a Greyhound bus and return in time for the fall school calendar. He had a cousin in San Francisco whom he had never met, but family was family after all and Manny, nee' Menachem, was a Berman and rumored to be doing quite well. Uri would write to him and hopefully he would have a place to stay. If not, there would certainly be many hostels and even camp sites. These were probably better lodgings than he had in the army, he said.

Upon learning the root cause of all this commotion, Morris scoffed at the story of Uri's alleged depravities. He ventured that every one of the peering eyes that caused all the *tsouris* had plenty of schnapps at home – *l'chaim!* As for Rabbi Friedlander, "*Achh,* a good fellow. I'm glad he was a *mensch* and didn't do worse by you. The man is between a rock and a hard place. It must be tough to try to keep your flock together when all the birds are flying the coop." Uri nodded in agreement at the rabbi's generosity and said that without it he couldn't even consider such a trip. Even with the paycheck, he would have to live like the poorest student.

Morris excused himself and rose from his seat, ambling into a room behind the counter. In a few moments, he reappeared carrying a tray of small teapots and cheerily announcing "*Ich kum!*" to the dining room. He stopped to visit the elders at each table, replenishing the Sweet N' Low packets and beaming with them in Yiddish before ultimately rejoining Uri at the table. Once seated, he pushed forward an envelope containing six one-hundred-dollar bills.

"Here, *boychik,* you can do me a favor with this. My son lives in Berkeley, it's only a bridge away from San Francisco. Bring him some money; he's always asking for it anyway. And keep two of those bills for yourself. I'll make you a care package too, to take with you, you shouldn't go hungry on such a long trip. You'll save me the bother of mailing my beautiful foods to him, the bottles always break from those klutzes in the post office. Go see him, he may even have a place for you to stay somewhere. He's a student at the University of California at Berkeley. *Nu? Sis a yiddishe kup*, yes? He was one of only two students from New Jersey to be accepted there. And *keneine hora*, he's a lefty like his granddad! Too big a *yiddishe kup* to pickle pastrami with his old man, who can blame him? My Nathan is out there to solve the world's problems. Maybe you can help him!" Uri stared at the envelope and knew his reflexive refusal would never be accepted.

*

A week later, Uri was on a Greyhound bus, staring at the endless vistas of the American nation. He watched the forests of Pennsylvania melt into the valleys of Ohio, the prairies of Nebraska, the mountains of Colorado and the deserts of Utah and Nevada, until he finally came to the familiar Mediterranean aspect of San Francisco bay. All the way there, through his four days and nights of cramped travel, he happily munched on delicacies that had been lovingly prepared by the Moonbeam Deli, and read three books that he had been meaning to get to. Every time he left their pages, he tried to think about the future, but every time did, it felt like thinking about the past.

As expected, Chava had been offered the position with Shalom Gadol. She began commuting to its New York office on the same day that Uri set out on his cross country trip. They shared the bus into the city and said their farewells in front of the Port Authority Terminal. The couple kissed goodbye long and hard, with the unsettling feeling that this was either the beginning or the end of something.

Uri assured Chava that he was looking forward to teaching again upon his return in the fall, and would be fine alone at home whenever she'd be away in her new job. He would of course miss her during her travels, but he would cultivate new hobbies and friends to fill the space, and with her new earnings, they'd finally be "getting ahead," as the Americans put it.

In turn, Chava assured Uri that she loved him no less now than ever before, and that she would write and call frequently whenever she was "on the road." Both realized simultaneously that neither of them fully believed what the other was saying. It was complex and disquieting new sensation that was foreign to the couple who had always been frank with each other. When they kissed goodbye, they didn't know for sure when, exactly, they'd see each other again.

As her husband disappeared into the terminal, Chava turned and faced the immensity of Manhattan. It was so dense, she marveled, how can this even be? Tentatively stepping onto Eighth Avenue, she saw two Hassidic men in passing and stopped them to ask directions to One Penn Plaza. Upon hearing her accent, they greeted her in Hebrew and exchanged pleasantries, leaving her with two business cards and an invitation to stop by their store anytime. Before walking a single block of her new world, she had already made two new friends.

*

The graffiti around the Greyhound terminal in San Francisco was a broad-scale canvas of peace signs and butterflies in day glow colors. Before leaving Paterson, Uri had managed to track down his cousin Manny, who lived in a part of the city called Castro and said he'd be thrilled to meet him. Uri had a plan worked out for his arrival. Before staying with his cousin, he would take the money and the remaining food from Morris

Blumenstyk and bring them to his son in Berkeley. He had been given the name of the campus organization where he could find young Nathan: Students For Social Rejuvenation.

Walking across leafy Sproul Plaza, Uri heard the sounds of hippies banging rhythms on plastic buckets as their friends danced in whirling-dervish circles. A veritable flea market of tables and soapboxes ringed the entire plaza, all touting various protests and demands: stop the war, burn the bra, free the oppressed. It was as if the many late-night debates at Beit Achdus had somehow spawned their own international movements, held right out in the open and with people actually taking notice, each issuing passionate calls for justices of every kind, all of it framed by the rich technicolor of this august and improbably beautiful setting.

A *real* setting thought Uri. This place was one of the crown jewels of the American university system, which he knew was one of the crown jewels of the world. This was not a small plot in the Galilee or a desiccating city in New Jersey. This was one of Western civilization's most hallowed intellectual centers. This was a place where history had been made, more than once, and might be made again on any given day. A new history, a history of the future. A gentle breeze from the Berkeley hills caressed his face and neck, which were bathed in an apricot light he had not seen since leaving Israel. He recognized immediately how at home he felt already. He had come to California. He had finally made *aliyah*.

$$\bullet \ \bullet \ \bullet$$

VENGEANCE IS MINE

"Any you guys know what happened to Mitch?"

There were no forthcoming answers to this plaintive question as it struggled to be heard over the swells of the Moody Blues. It was now nearly eleven and in fact no one had seen Mitch, a surprise given that this was the last party before the summer for the B'nai B'rith Youth Organization, Passaic and Bergen County chapters, circa 1972. All this action and Mitch was missing it!

The question was raised a second time, settling over a haze of Newport smoke and a tangle of crossed legs on the floor, and when there was no answer again, a suffix of concern was appended: "I hope nothing happened to him." This possibility made little impression on the room, which was presently engaged in a legion of offensive and defensive stratagems pertaining to amorous interest.

"He probably decided not to come. Maybe he had to finish his packing," offered Andy Simon, as he poured a too-foamy Genesee for himself and Lisa Margolis. "He's working at that camp for the summer."

This theory was left unchallenged and met with more silence, and as the song on the portable record player wound its way down, the music dissolved into solemnly intoned poetry. The teens listened closely, as if to a sage:

"Cold hearted orb that rules the night…"

"You figure he would have at least showed up to say goodbye," chimed Lloyd Markewitz. "That camp is in the back ass of nowhere. I couldn't even find the place on the map when he told me. Way out in the Adirondacks."

"Removes the colors from our sight…"

The most addled of the guests wondered what their sight would be like without colors. Would things look like the old black and white TV shows, or more like the confusing shades of the color blind? "Well it's his loss, we'll see him when he gets back," offered Andy, with little concern and less interest, as he turned his attention back to Lisa.

"But we decide which is right. And which is an illusion."

The music returned and built to a mighty crescendo. By the time it dissipated, several of the partygoers had already started necking.

At that moment, Mitch Klepper was huddled in a lonely Passaic alley with three other men, one of whom paced slowly at the entrance to Monroe St. All four were silent as they waited and waited – it had been more than an hour now – until the moment arrived at last. The lookout clicked his tongue and shot a glare to the others, who rose up as one and leaned into the building, deep in the shadows and well out of sight. Coming closer was the sound of several young men chattering in slurred Spanish. Mitch and his two mates hugged the darkness as the lookout called out in a friendly voice, "*Hola, pendejos* – say, who do you guys like to fuck first, your mothers, or each other?"

The three Puerto Rican men, fresh out of the nearby Estrella del Norte tavern, saw through their bleary eyes several salient details in this unlikely affront. First they saw a *blanquito* with the temerity to be walking around their neighborhood at this hour. Then they saw someone who'd be alone against three. Finally, they saw a wise guy who had insulted them thoroughly and without provocation.

What they didn't see was that there were three other men waiting in the alley, who immediately descended on them and began to beat them senseless with pipes and brass knuckles. Ambushed like this they were easy game, and bludgeoned within an inch of their lives, they soon made little noise. They did, however, leave a terrible mess of blood, missing teeth and broken bones. When the four assailants finished kicking the pulpy faces, they raced to a nearby car. Before it sped off in earnest, one of the men tossed a parcel in front of the Mercado San Juan storefront. In a moment, they heard a loud blast that shook the streets behind them and lit the rear view mirror in hellish shades of orange and red.

*

Not fifteen minutes later, Mitch was perched on an overstuffed divan in one of the last Victorians left on Pennington Avenue. From his vantage point in the parlor, he could see a peculiar cage elevator in the outer hallway, wrought in ornate gilded iron. This extravagant conveyance apparently existed to travel a meager route from ground level to an upstairs floor not twelve feet above. This must have been a grand old house in its day, thought Mitch, a *beautiful* house. Maybe a doctor's house, or a judge's.

There were no doctors here in this neighborhood anymore, he fumed, probably none left at all. The Blacks and the Puerto Ricans had driven them all away, this city is turning into a pit. Once upon a time this was probably a Jewish doctor's house, he decided, probably a specialist. How many Jews are left here in Passaic? Too many, according to the Blacks and the Puerto Ricans. Especially the Puerto Ricans. That's why we had to show them a lesson tonight. Maybe they need more than one.

The other men from the car were huddled across the room with their host, a portly man with a butcher's muscled arms and a tumbleweed beard. Satisfied with whatever conclusion they had jointly reached in their corner, they made themselves at home on the worn sofa and Rococo salon chairs. The host turned to Mitch and held out a glass of schnapps from a table tray.

"I hear you did very well tonight," he purred with warm pride, while the others nodded their agreement. "It needed to be done," answered Mitch, swallowing the fiery liquid in a single gulp. "Someone has to show them that we won't be taking their shit from them."

The three men who had been out with Mitch helped themselves to schnapps. The biggest one, who called himself Nuchem and had worked as the lookout, addressed Mitch, looking him straight in the eye. "That's exactly right, we won't be taking their shit anymore. Never again. This is our slogan and our vow: Never again. Never."

Turning to their host, he pointed his finger at him and asked, "You saw for yourself what happened here, in your nice little hometown, didn't you? How many days did they riot here, Mendel, burning and looting and destroying?" Their host didn't blink. "Three days. Three days a pogrom, and the goyim police did nothing." Nuchem nodded triumphantly as Mendel continued.

"A landlord has every right to evict tenants that don't pay their rent, does he not? Well? He gave the woman every chance, for months even, and they spit in his face. They laughed at the bloodsucker Jew landlord! One woman, with no husband, in an apartment with *eleven children*! I ask you, is this a family? A factory is more like it! These people are one step removed from living in the trees. When they finish eating their filthy *traif*, they throw their garbage right out the window into the back yard, where it stinks and draws vermin, and they don't care! They figure the idiot white people will clean up after them. They think it's the Jew landlord's problem, the one they don't have to pay the rent to. And when the police come to help the poor landlord evict the family of *twelve* who don't want to pay the rent – the *twelve* people living in a tiny one hundred dollar apartment – they riot and break the windows and rob the stores. For three days. Only the Jewish stores, of course. Then they mug and terrorize the few poor, old Jews who are left here that are unable to leave this city. A city that was once perfectly safe, but is now a jungle where they can't even leave their homes."

This speech elicited knowing nods from the others and poured premium grade fuel into Mitch's already seething outrage. "Whatever I can do to help," he announced to the others. "No one will protect us but ourselves." The others raised their glasses and offered a toast: "*l'chaim*. We will protect ourselves and our kind forever." The group clinked glasses and downed the liquor simultaneously.

*

The next day, Mitch was on an Amtrak train heading north through the thick green woodlands of upstate New York. As he watched the foliage melt into a kinetic blur, his hearing was completely focused on the relentless clacking on the train tracks.

This is what it would have sounded like, he thought, just like this. Clack-clack. Clack-clack. Over and over again. This would have been the hideous clacking drumbeat in the background for all those Jews, all those relatives and friends lost before he was born, as they gasped and prayed in the cattle cars and wondered what awaited them next. He could feel their anguish and fear, he could almost hear them, smell them. The stench must have been overwhelming he thought. Even now it filled his nose with an imagined déjà vu that made him shut his eyes in horror as the clack-clack, clack-clack hammered beneath his feet. Never again, he thought, never again. He would dedicate his life to it.

He was met at the train station by a strapping young man who introduced himself as Benji and whisked Mitch into a dusty station wagon. They drove for nearly an hour into the deep of the wilderness, past long-closed roadside stands and rusting billboards with Mohawk graffiti decrying the perfidies of the white man. Eventually they came to a nearly unmarked road and turned deeper into the thickets. Mitch could barely contain his excitement, even though the two had hardly spoken throughout the trip. Benji the driver had said only that he was glad to meet him and would leave all the talking for the orientation, which someone else would lead. Mitch said he understood and was satisfied to be silent.

They soon pulled up behind a grove of massive white pines that sheltered a campground of perhaps a dozen wooden cabins. These surrounded a grassy field accented with a flagpole, atop which flew the Israeli flag and below that, a banner with a fist raised heavenward atop the Magen David. Beyond the field, Mitch saw a dining hall packed with young people around his age, perhaps a bit older, boys and girls, men and women; he had apparently arrived during lunchtime. Benji took Mitch straight to his cabin and said he would fetch him in a half hour, when they'd both lunch together and he could meet Hiram, the camp leader, for his orientation.

It took only minutes for Mitch to empty his suitcase onto his appointed shelves. Evidently he was to share the cabin with three others, judging by the neatly made beds. A single window at the rear wall provided no light. It overlooked an enormous boulder not twenty feet away, practically the size of the cabin itself. The rock was covered with carvings and graffiti not unlike the banner on the flagpole; a fist over the six-pointed star. Oh well, not the homiest place he'd ever been, but whatever. He didn't know how long he'd be here. Maybe a few weeks, maybe the whole summer. It wasn't up to him, it was up to events. It was up to God, really.

There was dead quiet in the cabin, other than the rumbling from Mitch's empty stomach. His gut had been temperamental of late and outright testy since last night's violence. Especially after the argument they'd all had, or rather, the argument that one man was having with the rest of the crew. Or to be completely specific, the argument that the one man seemed to be having with Mitch. He was an uncle of Mendel, the stocky host of their getaway lair. The room's fervent conversation had been startled into momentary silence by the creaking upward ascent of the ornate cage elevator in the hallway. When it finally lumbered back to the ground floor, a bony, wizened man with an elegant silk robe and a walking frame wordlessly shuffled to the sideboard and helped himself to a glass of schnapps.

Spotting an unfamiliar face in the group, the man turned to his nephew with a gleeful smile and raised his glass. "Ah Mendeleh, *mazel tov*! I see you've found another poor schmuck for your shameful little fantasies!" Rolling his eyes,

Mendel muttered a profanity and turned to his guests with a helpless shrug. Switching his attention to Mitch, the man offered a toast: "*L'chaim*, young man! Welcome to the *mishpochah* of imbeciles. You now find yourself in the very best company with these righteous gentlemen, true *zaddiks* they are. There's no end of the good deeds you may accomplish. Please accept my best wishes, all of you, and the rest of your make-believe soldiers. Be fruitful and multiply. Only not in those words."

Mitch looked in amazement at his heckler and saw that neither Mendel nor the others were about to contradict anything. The man smiled broadly and continued, "No, don't look to them, *boychik*, they won't say a word. It's my house after all, yes Mendel? And I can't help that my very confused nephew, who lives here only by the generosity of his uncle, wants to pretend he is Goliath and not David, and wants to lose his soul so he can become a brute without a conscience. And I can't help that you probably want to pretend so along with him, yes? *Achh*, you are all a bunch of *pishers*. You are not what you think. You are nothing what you think."

Mitch could hardly stand to listen and felt duty bound to defend the group, even if at present they were staring sullenly at the floor or their drinks. "What do you mean, exactly," he demanded with considerable aggression. "We're imbeciles for wanting to defend Jews against violence?"

"No, *shepseleh*, you are imbeciles for believing that you are a solution, and not simply more of the problem. Violence begets violence, always, does it not? What did you do tonight? I don't want to know, but I know it was violence and it was not helpful. You did something bad, I'm sure. So, nu? Is it over now? Even-steven? Now that you did your bad thing, nothing bad will

Jews, but it is a self-perpetuating pathology. Because a Jew runs away, or because a Jew allows himself to be stepped upon, he guarantees that another Jew in the future will be attacked, because of the image that he has perpetuated. The JDL is creating a physically strong, fearless and courageous Jew who fights back. We are changing an image, an image born of two thousand years in exile, an image that must be buried because it has buried us. We train ourselves for the defense of Jewish lives and Jewish rights. We learn how to fight physically, because it is better to know how and not have to, than have to and not know how."

These words caressed Mitch like a cool summer breeze. At last, someone who understood!

The next day, Mitch found himself at a shooting range with a shotgun in his hands. It felt heavy at first, but after a few practice moves it was a natural appendage. Fifty yards away was a series of targets that he and six other inductees were to practice on. The images on the targets included an SS officer with a monocle, an Arab with a keffiyeh covering his face, and a Russian with a worker's cap and pointed goatee. The trainer had yet to provide Mitch and the other trainees with ammunition. Before doing so, he enjoined the trainees and a second group waiting their turn to have a seat and listen.

Parading left and right like a drill sergeant, he held up a formidable looking weapon and intoned, in a thick Brooklyn accent: "This is a twelve gauge shotgun. The most powerful weapon you'll ever need. It has an eighteen inch barrel, the shortest legal barrel you can buy in the United States." Mitch and the others listened closely, as if to a sage.

"This gun is capable of killing with seven shots; six shots in the magazine and one in the chamber. It's enough power to kill up to fifty people in a rapid-fire situation." Mitch tried to envision a situation where he'd have to kill so many people at once. He didn't think he'd lack the heart, just the manpower. There would probably be more than fifty people in any kind of rapid-fire situation. Would there be others along with him, shooting too? He hoped so, and scanned his campmates' faces to better assess their commitment. Would they be as cool under fire as he'd be? They'd better be.

*

The autumn light that falls over Paterson is richly beautiful, supplanting summer's flat yellow blanket with opulent, roseate shafts that might almost be Adriatic. Uncountable trees ring the city everywhere, even the downtown, even among the factories and smokestacks, these planted to hide the fearsome aspects of its dark satanic mills. The native Lenni-Lenapes enjoyed the view of its valley, and the great waterfalls of its river, from the nearby mountain they called Watchung and their conquerors finally called Garret. In October, the trees yield their chlorophyll to a timely passing and assume an impressionist's palette of maroons, ambers, vermilions and tangerines. The autumn air penetrates with crisp sensuality throughout the trees and the neighborhoods, no longer too hot to be outside, not yet cold or snowy. In these days, which bring the high holidays and the World Series, the back to school and the trick or treating, the city is at its most pleasant and serene.

Tucked into a quiet block on a quiet avenue in the quiet Eastside neighborhood was a small clapboard house that Mitch had been keeping his eye on. He was in the passenger seat of a Dodge Dart that had circled the block and cruised past the house several times in the past week. Nothing had changed from the first scouting. The same cars were parked in the same spots, the same woman next door walked her dog after dinner, the same downstairs lights flicked off around ten PM and the same upstairs light followed half an hour later. Once discerned, this pattern was tested and validated several times before both Mitch and Nuchem, the driver, felt sure of it.

This certainty was of the utmost importance to both of them, owing to an even greater certainty they'd only recently come to know. Their organization – by now, with hundreds of members, they could label themselves as such – had lately learned the whereabouts of the dread Nicolae Micandru, a sadistic officer of the Iron Guard who helped execute the horrific pogrom at Jassy in 1941 and later assisted the German section of the Romanian Security Services. He had apparently made it into the U.S. by changing his identity, seemingly more than once. His immigration papers falsely listed him as Mikolaj Kandruski, a Polish national; but now he was living right here in Paterson as Nicholas Andrews, passing as an ordinary good American, working as a lathe machinist. He was responsible for the merciless slaughter of thirteen thousand Jews, and thousands more deported to the camps. The scum had to die. It was more than about time.

A few nights later, well past midnight, the neighbor with the dog looked out her window to see what Marta was barking at. To her horror, she saw that the car parked out front, belonging to her neighbor, was presently engulfed in flames. Rushing out the door with her housecoat hardly buttoned, she ran next door, furiously slammed the doorbell and knocked as loudly as she could. *"Senor Nicholas! Tu carro! Este ardiendo! Senor Nicholas!"* Seeing his upstairs light go on, the neighbor waited until she heard Senor Nicholas begin a descent from the top of his staircase. Turning back to the street, she took several steps forward to survey the grisly site and put her hand to her mouth, thinking of the damage.

At that moment, a volcanic blast threw her forward, right into the burning car. Dazed and now nearly deaf, it took every ounce of her strength to roll back from the curb and onto the sidewalk. In the corner of her eye she could see a car slowly moving past the scene before speeding away. She looked at her left arm, which had been badly burned, but the worst pain was coming from her right arm, which was splattered with blood. Feeling around for a broken bone or whatever the source might be she found nothing. In an instant, she realized that the blood wasn't hers. A voice was screaming from the house behind her. She rolled over to see, and was greeted by a severed human foot not six inches from her face. She tried to scream herself but couldn't, she was starting to black out. The last thing she saw was the torso of Senor Nicholas writhing on the ground, both his legs blown off near the crotch.

The next day, Mitch was on a TWA jet to Athens, where he would then connect with El Al into Tel Aviv. As he stared out the window over the cloud-covered Atlantic, he was keenly appreciative of how quiet this trip was. The only sound to be heard beyond the soft conversations in distant rows was the otherworldly hum of the jet engines; unceasing and oozing with confidence and progress. There was no clack-clack, clack-clack here and there never would be. That sound had been erased and replaced with the sound of the new; this unhurried hum, remarkably serene, even with the jet engines roaring just outside. This gentle, patient, peaceful sound of progress must truly be the work of God.

Who but God could have given man the genius to fly when he has no wings? The genius, and the *will* to fly, so that man could overcome the limitations of what he has been, what he was born as? To be born a creature with no wings, but through God's genius and sheer human will, be able to fly nonetheless, and fly faster and further than anything God gave wings to! With God's help, anything was possible, anything could change, anything wrong could be made right, Mitch was sure of it. He had never been more sure of anything. He fell into a peaceful sleep to the lullaby of the roaring jet engines.

• • •

HELGA'S WAY

Early on a Tuesday morning, Helga saw the lights. They were beautiful beyond any words in her vast vocabulary. She stared at them in rapt wonder as wave after wave of brilliant beams surrounded her in perfectly symmetrical pairs, each alternating wildly between transparency and opacity, mating into ornate geometric filigrees spanning every direction, each birthing a thousand new translucencies in turn, all rendered in astonishing colors more intense than any she'd ever seen before, and some she'd never seen at all. They were all-engulfing, overwhelming; her heart began to race. They were more beautiful than the northern lights she once saw in Norway, or the Reims cathedral, or that sunrise over Bali. She felt herself giving over to them, letting her mind go, unfastening her amazement and melting passively into their incandescence; consenting to be one with them, submitting to their full totality. At which point, they began to fade and dissolve into ghostly wisps, as her vision slowly returned and a voice called her name. It was time for breakfast.

It was only Reggie, she realized, as the young man wheeled a tray over to her bed and warbled "Good morning, Helga my dear. Did you have a nice sleep?"

Oh no, was it only a dream? No, it wasn't, was it? Oh…well. Whatever it was, it was behind her now, she reasoned. Such a pity. If he only knew, If only she could tell him! But she couldn't. She hadn't been able to speak a word for more than a year, not since the stroke.

Reggie Dixon stirred up the farina and squeezed a bit of lemon into Helga's tea. Nobody really knew if she liked it that way, but he had once seen the outline of a smile when he'd asked, and from that day forward, the preference was assumed. In any case, Helga didn't complain. Frankly, she didn't do much of anything these days, but then, how much would you expect from a woman her age? Especially one who'd suffered a debilitating stroke that took away her speech and most of her motor skills? She had to be fed every day, cleaned every day, wheeled out of bed every day to "socialize" among the other residents of the Daughters of Leah nursing home.

The full extent of Helga's interactive ability was regretfully narrow, and quite subject to personal interpretation. It was true that she could often blink yes or no – the doctors had long understood that she could see and hear perfectly well, and that her cognition was seemingly intact. In fact, remarkably intact for someone who had suffered such a debilitating setback. She had been known to almost smile every now and again, or so it almost seemed, almost. Perhaps these were only the shadow of a tiny curl of the lips, or a perceived twinkle in her soft hazel eyes; again, much was open to subjective opinion.

Still frazzled by the apparitions, Helga took in her breakfast more slowly than usual. Reggie noticed this subtle shift and made extra sure that she was swallowing properly before moving to the next spoonful. He'd taken a shine to this silent spitfire ever since starting at Daughters of Leah, she was a bit of a good luck charm. She had been his first assignment, if that was the word, once management tried him at something beyond the simple patient transport he was hired to do.

He'd been fortunate to get this job. No employers had been in a hurry for a high school dropout with a rap sheet and a visible scar on his neck. Following a chastening and often harrowing six months in Rahway State detention, Reggie had taken to the word "reform" as a religion. In a rare lucky break, a well-liked aunt who worked in the Daughters of Leah kitchen had made a convincing plea for his case. He began at the bottom of the menial totem pole more than a year ago, but by now he was affectionately trusted and respected by staff and residents alike. He's got a talent with people, they'd say. He was on his way up in this business.

Helga swallowed her spoonfuls and tried not to dwell on what she was eating. What a crime, she thought. Someone with her palate, reduced to this pasty sludge, day in and day out. She, who had dined on *canard a l'orange* at Maxim's, and sukiyaki prepared by the personal chef of the Japanese Trade Minister. How sumptuous those meals were, so many of them, such wonderful times! She remembered now that she'd been to many of the most celebrated restaurants in the world, she and her crack teams from the Mirror-Gazette publishing company, for whom over the course of forty five years she'd worked her way up from typist to associate group publisher, the biggest title they gave to a woman at the time.

Indeed, she had been to five continents, as her award-winning magazine crews covered everything from scientific breakthroughs to fashion shows, the latest travel hotspots and culture – even the Beatles, before they broke in America, was that ten years ago yet? Ah yes, she had loved London so much, especially the curry. She could almost taste it, even now. Not this…dreck.

Reggie fed her tea through a straw to wash down her breakfast. As Helga sipped it, he marveled as always at the juxtaposition of onion skin frailty and immovable force that was staring back at him, always with that disarming half-twinkle. So tiny and so old, but still hanging in there, day after day, like a boxer that just won't go down. It was as if her exterior was slowly melting away and revealing an inner core made of stone, or steel. He'd never really thought much about what is was like to be old, to think so far into the future, not until he got this job, anyway. But ever since working with Helga, he thought of the future differently. It was as if her longevity had swung a door in his mind that he'd never bothered to open.

Would he, Reggie Dixon, live long and grow old? Well, maybe not Helga old, heh. But would he ever marry, become a father and a grandfather? Well…sure, why not? It wasn't long ago that he would have smirked or snarled at these blameless domestic notions. But he had turned his life around and was doing well now, they liked him here. More than one said he's a natural and has a future in senior care, which they predicted would be a huge industry one day. In a flash of precognition that lasted only milliseconds but was remembered forever, he suddenly saw himself at a podium in a suit and tie, lecturing a packed auditorium of attentive doctors and administrators. Reggie smiled down at Helga, who had finished her drink. Her mouth didn't smile back, but it didn't have to; he felt her affection clearly enough. He patted her hand gently. "You enjoy the rest of your morning, sweet pea."

Helga did not particularly enjoy the rest of her morning, nor did she mind it. Not that it was so different from any other morning since ending up here at Daughters of Leah. After the stroke, her daughter Danielle, coming all the way from that sheep ranch in outback Australia, had arrived to take charge of the situation, and it was she that put mom in this nursing home.

It had been quite an effort to reach her in Little Billabong. Mother and daughter had never been close. Helga's career left little time for a child all those years ago, and it was Morris, may he rest in peace, that wanted one in the first place. After Danielle was born, she was swiftly routed from nursemaid to au pair to day care to latchkey. When she was still a teen, she had already been caught shoplifting twice. After two desultory years at Vassar, she committed herself to living off the land and moved with another woman to the wilds of New South Wales, ten thousand miles from her unwanted past. News of her father's passing was eventually answered with a post card bearing the words "Sorry to hear, many condolences, I am well, hope you are too." It was the last correspondence Helga had from her daughter in years.

By the time Danielle got the word and made it back to America, her mother had been in the hospital for almost three weeks. The doctors and therapists tried valiantly to revive Helga's speech and movement, to no avail. There was no one to stand for her; she had outlived almost everyone she knew. It was only thanks to a neighbor with a key that they were able to find an address for the daughter. Danielle had arrived in Paterson, New Jersey, to the little brick house on the East side where her mother had inexplicably decided to spend her retirement after all those years in Manhattan, to find that Helga had organized her affairs with characteristic precision. Her mother's wishes were easy to follow, and a trust she had set up long ago would ensure a comfortable upkeep, should she ever need it. Now it was simply a matter of execution.

She could no longer take care of herself, so within a week of Danielle's arrival, Helga Greenfield was the newest resident of Daughters of Leah. Two weeks after that, the little brick house in Paterson was sold. The proceeds allowed Danielle to finally leave the sheep ranch so she could move to Sydney with her new boyfriend Aryeh, whereupon she soon became a stepmother and soon after that, a step grandmother. Her shy suggestion of the name "Helga" for the new baby was met with delighted and unanimous family approval. Helga the elder would have loved this improbable turn of events, had she ever learned of it.

As it was, she was feeling a bit bored today. This would ordinarily be a given for someone in her condition and situation, but Helga wasn't usually bored; in fact, quite the contrary. She had a vivid and nearly infinite archive of glamorous experiences to reflect back on, here in her silent state. She had lived a remarkable life and had a formidable memory, and in her forced quietude, she replayed movie upon movie of all the exquisite times, momentous and minute. Trapped in herself as she was, in her body and age, she now had the time and the wisdom to savor these memories again and again, to dissect them, to understand and appreciate them even more deeply and fully than when they actually occurred. These recollections were the enjoyable daily entertainment of Helga's life, but this morning, they just didn't seem enough. The lights were more interesting to think about.

*

After breakfast, an orderly wheeled Helga into the activity room, which was generally notable for its dearth of activity. Sadie, as usual, was working fruitlessly on the same jigsaw puzzle as every day. Sarah was already asleep in her wheelchair, and it looked like Bernie and Adele would soon join her. Esther and Frida were in their usual positions, staring out the window while chatting together, and Fred was pushing his walker around the circumference of the room, like an endless second hand on a timeless clock.

When Helga was steered into her usual spot, she noticed someone new in the room, or rather heard her. Slumped in a wheelchair and deep in tears was a new resident, a woman whose dyed auburn bun bobbed in sync with each heavy sob. She was inconsolable, as two successive attendants fretfully concluded. Fearful that her crying would upset the other residents, an orderly turned her chair and began wheeling her out of the room. When the woman caught a look at Helga, tiny and withered and staring at her with unblinking eyes, she wailed loudly, her anguish echoing in the room long after she was gone.

Such was the usual way when a new resident came in, thought Helga. Goodness, what were they expecting? This is the final stop, of course. There isn't a future here, only the past, and spending quality time with the past is what makes the present at Daughters of Leah bearable, even pleasurable, am I right? And these others, the ingrates, with so much to be thankful for, besides! To still be in control of one's body, to be able to walk, have a conversation, hold a book – these are gifts at our age, not to be taken for granted!

Helga wished she could walk, or speak, or read a book. For a few weeks, one of the new nurses had read aloud to her and that was wonderful, despite its being the Ladies Home Journal, a hated competitor to Modern Homemaker magazine, which she and her team had launched with great success in the wake of the GI Bill and the mass migrations of families to the suburbs. The young nurse eventually tired of the one-sided ritual, not knowing if Helga was following her words or even hearing them. After a while, she just felt self-conscious and stopped. Helga missed it and wished she could say so, but alas.

Instead, she played and replayed her considerable mental archives, every day, all day, and incredibly, it was enough. It was as if she had catalogued all her experiences and now had the leisure to browse them at will, grazing here, binging there; vividly re-living a life that had taken her to some of the world's most rarified places and moments.

She had climbed newly discovered pyramids in Guatemala, broken bread with Nobel Prize winners in Stockholm, sipped champagne on the deck of the Queen Mary, was gifted with a piquet and taffeta evening gown straight from the workshop of the great Balenciaga. These and other museum-quality recollections were reliable entertainment until lunch time, and from after lunch until nap time, and then into the evenings, when it would soon be time for dinner and then for bed. Such were the rhythms at Daughters of Leah. There was little else she could do, other than enjoy them.

*

This being a Tuesday, most of the residents were eventually led, cajoled or wheeled into the recreation room, where there was a piano and a small stage area where volunteers would provide performances and lectures. Today, there sat behind the scuffed baby grand a slender, well-greyed man, not so much younger than his audience. When given his cue, he shyly introduced himself as Gil Buckbinder, saying it was his privilege to play for your pleasure, and that he'd be happy to take any requests.

Accepting the silence in return, Gil turned to the keyboard and began to play slowly, softly, in a pensive key that plainly exposed his mood. He glanced up at the residents, few of whom seemed to be paying attention anyway, and wondered why he was here after all. Was it a spirit of giving? Simple love of music and performance? Nothing better to do on a Tuesday? God no, please let it not be that.

His left hand repeated a meandering figure while his right hand flitted around for a melody. Looking up at his audience again, he wondered how long it would be before he'd be sitting out there in a place just like this one, one day too soon. Maybe listening to the piano player, maybe not. Maybe all there upstairs, maybe not. His heart sank. He missed Ruth so much. Life was nearly unbearable since she passed away.

He noticed the tiny old woman in the wheelchair planted nearby, staring at him frankly, penetratingly. He realized that he hadn't actually begun to play anything coherent yet, so he plinked a few more notes over the bass line, hoping something would catch.

No rush, he supposed, this isn't the most sophisticated audience, or the most attentive. In a lengthy career as a jazz pianist and arranger, Gil had played many impressive shows, so if this wasn't one of them, well, no big deal. He'd toured more than once with the legendary Bucky Pizzarelli, his longtime pal from Eastside High, and even backed Les Paul for two weeks at the Village Vanguard. That was where he first met Ruth, sitting at a table near the stage and gazing at him from the audience with a smile he never forgot. While it was considered woefully uncool by his bandmates, he'd practically sprinted from the dressing room after the set, hoping that the pretty brunette with the glasses might still be in the club. He didn't get past the corridor before running into her, as she'd been waiting for him, and from that moment forward, they were inseparable for the next twenty four years. God, he missed her so much.

Gil looked out at the room again and imagined he was back in that smoky venue, all those nights ago. He remembered where Ruth had been sitting, nursing a Bloody Mary, just off stage left. Moving his eyes there and expecting a ghost, he saw the tiny woman again, still staring as before. He plinked a few more attempts at a theme before one of them finally stuck.

It was the intro to a lovely haunting melody of his, written long ago, made of thick, ambivalent chords. Not quite major, not quite minor, it had always been one of his favorite motifs and he couldn't remember the last time he played it. Its inner voices implied everything while declaring nothing, not until the next set of chords would almost settle things, at least for another few bars. It was this very tune, called "Hoping You," that the Shecky Freeman Orchestra had built an entire suite around, back when Gil was the arranger. They'd played the Catskills all those summers ago, and had toured as far as Buffalo and Cleveland, how many years ago was that now?

As his playing built momentum, Gil lost himself deeper into the music. To each melodic question he played a selection of answers, equally ambivalent in their turn. It was as if the sound of indecision was the point. Of course he had structured it this way, back in the day, so that each of the soloists could choose which way to roll when their turn came around. Especially their ace clarinetist Hank Morton, who ended up with a nice career and was now an executive with Columbia Records. Today, in the rec room of Daughters of Leah, there were no soloists, there was only Gil. Where the tune would go was entirely up to him.

He shifted the melody down to his left hand and then seemingly out of nowhere, struck a fine, clear, penetrating chord of uplift with his right. Its harmonics bounced throughout the low-ceilinged room, causing pearly overtones that lingered in long, impressionistic reverberations. It was a genuinely sublime moment of sound, beautiful like a bell, indescribable in words; the kind of moment that so many composers and musicians live for. Gil knew it and felt it immediately and smiled, and closed his eyes in a kind of grateful rapture before looking up to see if anyone else had felt it. Nobody was really paying much attention except Helga, who continued to stare at him, with a seeming twinkle in her eyes. She almost looked as if she were smiling.

Gil smiled back at her. He struck the chord again and waited for the wonderful overtones, then improvised on top of them. He remembered playing this tune so many different ways over the years, how did it go back then? He recalled with a grimace that the piece had been so poorly abridged on the one record that he and Shecky's orchestra had cut, back in '55. They'd left out the best parts, dammit, what were they again?

As if moved by an outer body intelligence, his hands began to play music that he hadn't heard in decades. It suddenly came back to him as effortlessly as breathing, and it flowed out of him in ascending modulations that shone brighter with each succeeding measure. It was spellbinding enough to make the staff members stop what they were doing and listen.

As he wound down the tempo to end the piece, he realized he was a different man than the one that had sat down at the piano not five minutes ago. He decided right then and there that he'd work to finally expand "Hoping You" into a full, finished suite and he'd make a beautiful orchestration of it besides. So many different ways he could go with it! He had time for that now. And he still had his friends in jazz circles, even Hank over at Columbia. Maybe they'd be interested in it, they might even record it. He'd dedicate the piece to Ruth, she would have loved that.

Closing his eyes, he finished playing and savored for a silent moment both his late wife's memory and his excitement for the future. The residents who could applaud started clapping loudly, as did all of the onlooking staff members. Gil looked up at their appreciation and was inexpressibly moved. He felt Ruth's smooth hands on the back of his shoulders and her cool, soft kiss on his temple. He looked out to where she sat all those years ago, just off stage left, and saw the tiny old woman still staring at him with that funny hint of a smile.

*

Helga was exhausted by the time she was wheeled back into her room. Goodness, you really do get tired so early when you're old, she chuckled to herself. Once upon a time, right about this hour would be when she and Morris would finish dressing for a quick bite at the Russian Tea Room before walking next door to join friends at Carnegie Hall. After that, they'd all head to the Carlyle or the Rainbow Room for a nightcap before she'd dreamily watch the neon of Times Square rise and recede on the taxi ride down to their Greenwich Village townhouse.

Ah, she missed those days, all those people, all gone now. It made her a bit heartsick. Poor Morris, nobody would have guessed he'd pass so young. At least it was quick and peaceful; one morning poof, he just didn't wake up. Helga had always hoped she'd pass the same way, but it had now been more than a year of not passing since those first terrifying moments of the stroke. At this stage, she looked at her longevity as a competitive sport that she was good at and winning. She certainly didn't like being fed and washed like an infant, and ignored by the staff, even though she could hear everything they said perfectly well. But with the Museum of the Inner Helga providing an endless source of entertainment, she was content to go on.

She had long become used to being alone, though never actually lonely. No one really understood why she left her chic Greenwich Village home and relocated to Paterson all those years back. Long ago she had inherited the small brick house on Derrom Avenue where she'd grown up, and for all those years had preferred renting it over selling. After Morris passed, she decided it'd be a perfectly fine place to live out her retirement. This opinion was notably amplified when a realtor friend explained the emerging laws for New York co-op and condo conversions, and told her how much her charming townhouse on Barrow Street could now fetch on the open market. Helga had taken the cash, which was considerable, and simply relocated herself in the house where she was raised, across the Hudson river, just fifteen miles away.

For Helga, it was like moving to the country. She now had a back yard and a flower garden, and enough room for a pair of poodles, which she had always wanted. She had a washer and dryer and air conditioning, even a dishwasher, all of which had been out of the question in her quaint 19th century building and its prehistoric wiring. She now lived just a brief stroll from the sculpted Eastside park, where she took Salt and Pepper for daily romps off the leash while she read the Times on a favorite bench. She never lost her New Yorker's indifference to cars and never got a driver's license. Instead, she was ferried everywhere by an armada of Jiggett's taxis, often hiring one into Manhattan to see a Broadway show or attend a dinner party. She spent her retirement years mostly by herself, in happy solitude, doing what she loved best and what she always wanted to do – learn to paint, read great books and relax. After forty five years of breakneck pressures with Mirror-Gazette, she felt she deserved it.

Paterson and a back yard may have been a move to the country for Helga, but for her friends it was more like another planet. They jokingly told her nobody would ever come visit her in New Jersey, and after a few exceptions, the prophecy was self-fulfilling. Only her best friend Joan made the trip with any regularity. The two would spend weekends together laughing and drinking velvety French wines and savoring artful confections from Balducci's, while they dueled madly at Scrabble and dissected the world around them deep into the nights. She missed Joanie most of all; it was only after she passed away too that Helga began to feel as if she might really be lonely. Not long after, the stroke showed her convincingly that loneliness comes in many shapes and sizes, with none of them made to measure.

*

It was near the end of the year, and the Daughters of Leah staff had already put out the Chanukkah decorations for the festival of lights. The residents always found these adornments cheering, and they greeted each new evening of the holiday with gladness as another bright orange bulb joined the others on the electric menorah. Tonight would be no exception to the spirit of the season, as the entertainment would again be provided by The Lightengales, a folk trio singing traditional Jewish songs.

The residents had already taken their places in the audience, with only a few stragglers now being wheeled in. Helga was among them; she had woken from her nap more heavily than usual. A nurse steered her to a colleague at the end of a row and pulled up a chair flanking Helga's other side. They were both so protective of her. It was as if they were daughters.

Seated alone, a few rows in front of them, was the new woman with the auburn bun. Her name was Eva Dankner, but none of the residents knew this. She hadn't made any friends yet; in fact, she'd hardly spoken to anyone since coming here. She never wanted to be in this place, never wanted to leave home. But what choice had there been, after all? Her children had no room for her; where would the grandkids sleep? After Pop-Pop passed, everyone tearily agreed that Daughters of Leah would be the best solution for grandma. The kids and grandkids assured her they'd visit all the time. An hour after her admittance and being left to her room, she'd started crying and had barely stopped for two days.

She wasn't like these others, with one foot in the grave, she sniffed. She was still lively and vivacious, at least most of the time, even if she was a little confused now and again – who wasn't? The falls, they were accidents, they could have happened to anyone! And now, because of the stupid accidents, she's ended up here in a nursing home, doomed to stare at the walls with these others who are on their way out. To have no one to talk to and just wait for the end to come. She lowered her head and tried to stop herself from sobbing again.

The Lightengales had taken the stage and warmly greeted the room as they tuned their guitars. The titular Gale chatted pleasantly about holidays at her home and how her youngest had just lit his first Chanukkah candles only the other night, and what a special memory it would be for her, and for him; to be cherished together forever. Memory is a kind of forever, she reminded them, maybe the best kind. Then she and her mates eased into a lovely three-part arrangement of *Ma'oz*

Tzur, explaining for the benefit of the gentiles in the audience that this translated to Rock of Ages. Their voices weaved in and out of each other with grace and easy precision; they'd been singing together for years.

Eva looked up from her doldrums as they vocalized, and in these three women she instantly saw her own granddaughters. They had been singing together in just this way for a few years now, ever since they heard the Mamas and the Papas and the Beach Boys on the radio and had become transfixed. Eva remembered the joy on their dimpled faces as they harmonized during little concerts they'd stage for the adults, singing "God Only Knows" and "Dream a Little Dream of Me." The intensely vivid recollection of those beautiful little faces, at those beautiful crystalline moments, with those beautiful sounds, seemingly playing out right now in front of her, sent a palpable jolt of warmth down Eva's spine and even her soul. Bless the Lightengales, they were making her feel a little better.

The applause at the end of the song was quiet but sincere. One of the nurses' aides, whose crush on the lone unmarried Lightengale dated back to last year's concert, was perhaps too enthusiastic with his loud whistle from the back of the room. Eva turned around to see where the improbable noise came from, and as she did, she saw the face of the tiny old woman that had previously shocked her into tears and made her so depressed.

Now, as then, the face stared at her unblinkingly, but this time, Eva firmly decided she would not look away. The two nurses flanking Helga offered friendly smiles, hoping the new resident was finally edging out of her shell. Eva stared back at Helga, and suddenly she felt awful about her recoiled reaction of the other day. She realized how insulting it must have been, even if she couldn't help it. She gave Helga a small smile of apology before turning back to the stage. She would find an appropriate moment to introduce herself and apologize for real. There would be plenty of time.

The Lightengales segued into *David Melech Yisrael* and invited the audience to sing along. There were no takers that could be heard above a mumble, but Eva remembered all five words and began to join them. She had a sweet, lilting voice that had sung in the synagogue choir, long ago when she was a girl. It was she, after all, the music lover in the family, that had introduced her granddaughters to the genius of the Andrews Sisters and the Chordettes. She hadn't sang out loud in years, and as her voice grew in volume and confidence over the song's tumbling repetition, she realized that this really felt wonderful. The Lightengales smiled back at her from the stage and stopped their guitars for a few rounds of *a cappella*. Switching to guitar accompaniment, they even coaxed a solo verse from Eva, which delighted the entire room.

When the song was over, the audience applauded the Lightengales, who graciously pointed to Eva, and in a moment, the room was applauding her as well, in both appreciation and welcome. Eva turned around to witness this turn of events and realized that yes, the room was actually applauding her. Another jolt of warmth, louder than the first one, went down her spine and her soul again; she teared up. Scanning the faces, she landed on Helga's, still staring, but now with a small glint in her eyes.

*

While her band tuned up again, Gale turned to storytelling. As she entertained the room with tales from her recent trip to Israel, Helga was in a more prickly mood than usual. The holidays always evoked mixed feelings from her. Her parents were deeply assimilated and non-observant. She had never been at all religious, and had fought for much of her life to be taken seriously in a deeply competitive world as a person, as a woman, as a professional, as a mentor; as something more than just a Jew. Anyone can be born a Jew, but not any Jew could become Helga Greenfield. This much she knew and believed.

And yet, here she was at Daughters of Leah, a Jewish nursing home, spending her last days among generally Jewish residents, and here because…why? Simply because she was Jewish? She had nothing in common with any of these people. She hardly been to a temple since her wedding, and only then because Morris insisted. These women here, look at them; they were the widows of fabric salesmen and electrical supply wholesalers and fruit purveyors, among other upstanding but unambitious tradesmen of the locality. They were women who lived their entire lives within their homogenous Jewish neighborhoods – new world *shtetls*, Helga had always called them – without a care in the world beyond their families and homes. What on earth did she have in common with these people? That they were all born into the same religion? What a broad brush, what a reduction. She wished she could say so out loud.

Then she remembered the less-social residents here, the handful like Klara and Sabina and Moniek, who had made it out of Europe somehow, and whose families had brought them here for their final years specifically *because* it was a Jewish facility and that's where they'd feel most comfortable. They formed closed circles where they'd speak together in Yiddish, effectively creating yet another *shtetl* within their four walls.

Helga had nothing in common with these people either, other than a shared possession of an ancient bloodline. She had never been ashamed of her Jewishness, but was never out front with it either. She was an American that happened to be a Jew. But just now, looking across the room at Moniek and Klara, she realized with a start that they had probably said exactly the same thing themselves, all those years ago, back in the old country:

I am a German – or a Pole, or Czech, or whatever – that happens to be a Jew.

Gazing at them as they happily followed the storyteller, she saw in that moment how fragile such a stance could really be. How illusory. She had nothing in common with these people, true enough, but that was only in one plane of understanding. What if there was another plane where she had everything in common with them after all, maybe the most crucial thing? She'd never thought to consider it, until just this moment.

Gale finished her story about the lovely beaches of Tel Aviv, and the Lightengales launched into *"Dreidel, Dreidel, Dreidel."* Nothing could have made Helga's mood more sour. Ugh no, no, no, *please*…not this children's song! Again! Are we children? Is this what we're reduced to? Can't they see how condescending this is? Underneath her silent, motionless exterior, Helga was fuming. But gaily chirping and making hand-spinning motions, the Lightengales encouraged the audience to sing and clap along.

Sadie clapped spastically and arrhythmically from the front row, grinning like a two year old. Well, that's about par for her, thought Helga. Eva, the new woman, was singing softly but clearly, self-harmonizing with the singers on the stage. The rest of the audience simply smiled politely, all except Helga, who would have scowled if she could. First she was just an old person, then she was just a Jew, now she's just a child. Ugh, this silly, degrading children's song again! Dear God, make it stop, please just take me now! Just at that moment, she started seeing wild, vivid colors in the corner of her eye.

Soon the Lightengales were ready to finish their set. They told everyone how happy they were to perform this evening and that they wished the brightest of holidays to everyone during this, the festival of lights. And now they will conclude with the beloved national anthem of Israel and of the Jewish people. Please sing "*Hatikvah*" along with us!

By the time this request had been made, Helga had been deep in the embraces of the beautiful lights. They were more stunning than the time she saw the Milky Way in South Africa, or that double rainbow above Niagara Falls, or the crazy light show in that 2001 movie that she and Joanie, the two little old ladies in the balcony, had gotten high to see. They were all encompassing, overwhelming. Helga began to lose awareness as the Lightengales sang, while the two nurses flanking her sang along and translated:

> "*Kol od balevav penimah...*
> As long as in the heart within..."
> "*Nefesh yehudi ho'miyah…*
> a Jewish soul yearns..."

The lights grew so intense that they lost all quality of color, ascending upward into pure white luminance that danced around her in curling geometric filigrees. The song continued its call of hopeful longing, but Helga could barely hear it now. She struggled to maintain her senses, her vision was fading fast. She felt she was leaving this world and that she was, perhaps, meeting God at last. Soon, the lights took over, and with her hearing now the final link to her earthly existence, Helga directed the last of her strength toward the increasingly beautiful music, which was now synchronized with the lights, trying her best to join them too, to be one with them both. A sound came from her tiny throat, hoarse, croaking, and completely unexpected:

"*Yehhh..roo…shlime…*"

"Oh my God, Helga, did you SAY something?" The other nurse heard it too. "What? What did you say, Helga?" She patted her hand while the other nurse motioned for the doctor. "Oh my God, did she say *Yerushalaim*? *Jerusalem*? Did you hear that? She spoke! Helga, you spoke!" But Helga couldn't hear them anymore. She was already waltzing with the lights.

• • •

FALLING UP

Everything seemed so miraculous at just this moment, but it was the breathing that struck Stanley Luskin as the most miraculous of all, the purest and most dazzling expression of the miracle of life. As he watched his infant daughter dozing peacefully on his lap, he marveled at her every breath with a novel emotion hovering precisely between serenity and awe. Every tranquil breath feeding the precious oxygen into her tiny body, diligently transporting it from nose to lungs and her heart, and from there to everywhere else – it was all so effortless, so elemental. So beautiful. He stared at her contentedly, as if there was nothing else in the world.

He tried to remember the scientific terms for the component parts of this life-giving oxygenation process. Something fusion. He had learned them years ago, back during his one year-plus of pre-med study at Farleigh Dickinson University; his three semesters of biology, general and organic chemistry, physics, mathematics and calculus, psychology, sociology and statistics, among other classes, little of which stuck then and less of which stuck now. The temporal demands of so many courses had been daunting enough, he remembered, especially the lab work. But if he were to be honest, it was really the intellectual demands that were frankly too much for him, putting an end to this particular avenue of Stanley's future. It was easier to admit this now than back when he was eighteen; after all, not everyone is cut out to be a doctor. Not even if his parents always told him he'd one day be a doctor.

He had enrolled in the pre-med program at age seventeen with no great enthusiasm nor any regrets. It was just something that was expected of him, or more charitably, anticipated for him. In all the times as a young boy that he pictured himself with a white coat and stethoscope, or when it had been pictured for him by others, he rarely stopped to imagine the full set of processes and milestones that would be necessary to realize such a plan. Becoming a doctor was just something one did and could do, like being a lawyer, or an accountant, or any other profession. At least one could here in America. At least it had seemed that way to his immigrant parents, which is to say his refugee parents, or more specifically, his survivor parents, neither of which had the opportunity for much education before the war. Both regretted this as a minor lacking among the many other misfortunes they and theirs had suffered in the old country, but it was keenly felt nonetheless.

When they arrived in America with a two-year old daughter – Stanley's older sister Esther, now an orthodox rabbi's wife in Brooklyn – they quickly took as unassailable truth that here in America – *mit'n adukation* – anyone could become anything. And a doctor in the family? Why not? His mother's great-uncle Herschel of blessed memory, he was a doctor in Szeged before the war. Why not the great grandnephew? Why not indeed? Someone may have asked this very question the day Stanley was born at Barnert Hospital, four years later.

Absorbing the simplicity and certainty of such a plan, imparted by the only role models he'd ever really known, Stanley never thought much about his accountability in this scheme. He assumed he'd simply step into the shoes of the physician-to-be when the right time came in his life. That would be much later, when he'd be grown up, or mostly. He was therefore not dissuaded by being an emphatically average student from the moment he entered school.

Working from the premise that being as good as the average student was actually pretty good, all things considered, Stanley was not discontent with his adequate performance. His parents did not feel this way. They cajoled and wailed and struck and did all they could to extract greater academic talent from their youngest, but at the end of the day, they thought more of his aptitude than was perhaps wise or realistic. Stanley never wanted to disappoint them, and so he never let on that maybe he wasn't cut out to be a doctor. Perhaps because he hadn't realized it himself until he started flunking out.

Well, that was a long time ago, he thought, as he watched his daughter breathe, and felt lovely waves of serotonin coursing through his own body, keeping perfect time with her miniature respirations. It was as if they were in sympathetic resonance, a term he suddenly remembered from the forgotten classes. He made a mental note of the sensation and hoped that he could and would feel it again and again, for as long as his daughter lived with him. As he focused on the synchrony he was now sharing with his baby girl, it reminded him of the mirroring exercises they taught him in his theater classes, back when he thought that acting might be his real calling.

He had really enjoyed that time, for a time. As his fourth semester of school had already been paid for, Stanley was duty bound to finish his second year of college with classes of some kind. The credits from a few easy electives would come in handy when he figured out what he really ought to study, at which point he would simply return to school. An inviting smile in the cafeteria from a lissome theater major, swathed in a peasant blouse and batik skirt, decided the details for him and resulted in Stanley's first girlfriend as an adult. She was charming and light and curious and happy, proving the adage that opposites really do attract.

Ah Antonia, he sighed – what a crazy time! He was the taboo Jewish boyfriend of her Catholic school daydreams, until the day he wasn't. She lived with several other theater students in a rented house in Teaneck, near the main street and Bischoff's ice cream, where they'd hold court and read *Variety* and imagine their names in lights.

This merry band of Broadway and Hollywood stars in the making was friendly and accepting of Stanley. For him, it was like finding a new family. Thanks to their encouraging words, disproportionately felt through sheer unfamiliarity, he tried out for a minor part in a graduate production of "The Importance of Being Earnest." Because it was such a small role, he ended up getting cast. He invited his parents to the premiere, but neither would come. The curtain call was the first and only time anyone ever clapped for him.

Over the Christmas break, after another stormy outburst from his apoplectic father that "this place isn't a hotel," Stanley packed his clothes and moved in with Antonia and the others. His parents were aghast and scared to death of where he'd be living and with whom, and why he wouldn't he coming home anymore, and what would he do for food and money, and how could he be doing this to us, who have been through so much?

It took a certain amount of *chutzpah* for Stanley to make this move, as he really didn't know what he'd do for food and money, and he knew his parents would never understand or appreciate a direction so, well, what was the word? *Bohemian.* To them, Bohemians were Austro-Hungarians that were almost German or almost Czech or Slovak; this is something to aspire to? It was a hard parting between parents and son with much handwringing, and it's likely that Stanley's father never forgave this exodus, not for the rest of his life. Nonetheless, Stanley soon found himself in love for the first time, living gloriously as a bohemian with a lower case b in a house with six other students, working as a waiter at Old Salt in Paramus and going into New York for auditions.

Despite his inexperience and the odds overall, one of these auditions actually resulted in his being cast. It was an off-off-Broadway production of an avant-garde play written by a minor member of the Andy Warhol orbit. The director thought Stanley's suburban look was perfect, and his New Jersey accent would lend just the right authenticity to the part.

In his still impressive naivete, Stanley thought the gang would be thrilled for him, but none of them were. They said the right things for a moment, but a sense of irritated jealousy precluded much more, and even Antonia began to cool after that wonderful first night when he'd told her the news. The idea that Stanley – with a grand total of one semester of classes and no prior ambition or interest to become an actor – could be getting parts in a New York production dismayed them to their core. It shook their confidence that training, talent and hard work were more important than luck. Maybe this was not so.

Whether organically or out of esprit de corps, Antonia soon veered to the group's disdain over Stanley 's quick ascent.

She joined the others when they mocked the ephemeral nature of the Warhol experiments, judging that they weren't really theater, and how it wasn't really possible to do good work with amateurs anyway. Stanley was puzzled by their attitude until he understood it a little better, and to counteract their objections, he gamely rehearsed his few lines longer and harder than was really necessary. When the show premiered some weeks later, in a Soho garage smelling of motor oil and disinfectant, Antonia and her eventual next boyfriend came for the first night. After that, nobody did. The show – not really a play, but a conceptual take on a play – went nowhere, got no reviews, gained no audience and quickly disappeared as if it never happened. It left Stanley with the very disconcerting feeling that this kind of thing happens a lot to actors.

My goodness, that surely was a crazy time, he thought, a stupid time, in retrospect. He wondered what ever became of Antonia? He vaguely thought she'd gone to Hollywood, but that might have been his own mythologizing. More likely she's divorced from a white shoe attorney in Larchmont and scouting a next husband in the Hamptons. Thinking back, he didn't feel charitable toward her, even though she had made him a man, in the carnal vernacular. In the aftermath of their breakup, having lost the first love of his life, he'd felt toyed with and used. When she'd had enough of her Jewish boyfriend who had the temerity to get cast off-off Broadway, she simply went cold and moved on.

This sour turn of events not only left Stanley with his first broken heart, but also presented an acute problem with his living situation. He couldn't stay with the troupe anymore, and moving back in with his parents, into their small Empress House apartment with its perpetual scent of boiled chicken, would be too claustrophobic, not to mention mortifying. It was time to strike out into the world, so in order to pay for a tiny and not altogether safe apartment in Paterson's crumbling mill district, he bumped up his waitering duties and signed his first lease. In addition to working the dinner slot at Old Salt, he now added some late shifts at the Forum Diner, which left him with about ten hours a day to sleep and do everything else in his life.

Well okay, that was a crazy time, and yes, also a stupid one, Stanley agreed with himself. Why did he do it? Because a girl in a peasant blouse would consent to have sex with me? It seemed absurd now. How many hours, days and weeks of waiting tables did that sex end up costing? He grunted a mirthless chuckle. Without Antonia and the troupe in his life, his interest in acting had flickered and died with indecent celerity. Now left with no marketable skills beyond jotting down an order and keeping the coffee cups filled, he holed himself up in his apartment during the ten hours off his feet and tried to figure out where his life would, should, could and need to go next.

It was maybe too late to go back to school. What would he study, after all? The shock of being insufficient material for a doctor was easily repeated in the consideration of other callings that had been posited on his behalf, notably the legal profession. A research trip to the library confirmed this fear and scared him out of a few other directions besides. He wasn't good enough at math to be an accountant, or good enough at learning to be a teacher. He wasn't connected to anyone with money, so opening a business wasn't in the cards, even if such a plan would be in his wheelhouse, which it wouldn't.

Lost for ideas, he met with an academic advisor from school. In assessing the emerging opportunities for young men in today's economy, the counselor suggested computer programming. Stanley had barely heard of computers and thought they were machines that the FBI used to spy on people. The counselor advised him that computers were becoming smaller and more widely employed, and there would be a great need for software (what a word!) programmers. This was something that Stanley could study right here at FDU. They'd accept all his accumulated credits straight away.

To Stanley, this all sounded wonderful, if a bit cloudy. He didn't know anything about computers, or machines in general, for that matter. He did know that he needed a new direction and fast. His feet hurt after the long evenings and nights waiting tables, and his car was molested more than once outside his Oliver Street apartment. He went deep into his savings, such as they were, but it was not enough to make tuition at private Farleigh Dickinson University. On the other hand, thanks to the modest fees of the local state school, he could begin almost immediately at nearby William Paterson College. Unfortunately, not all of his prior credits would be deemed transferable in this exchange. As a result, what should have been his third year of college became instead his freshman year, studying what was not yet called computer science.

From the very first, he was even more shocked by the coursework than he had been with pre-med. Applied mathematics! For someone who had to repeat Algebra in high school because he just didn't get it, the future looked worryingly obtuse. Stanley approached this problem the way he did every other, by simply working longer at it. Learning eventually came in dribs and drabs, but when he finally understood one lesson well enough, the rest of the class was deep into the next, or the one after.

What were these crazy things after all, and what good were they? Algorithm design, complexity assessments, parsing, compiling, translation – what did it all mean? Why were there different languages and why didn't they talk together? Which one should he learn, which one would get him a job? And what kind of human can actually keep up with all this? He'd often stare at the measly lines of code he was able to author or paste and wonder how long it would take to really master Fortran or COBOL, and whether either would still matter by the time he did. For every ounce of emotional stability that Stanley gained for having picked a path, he lost two more to the aching fear that it wasn't the right one. Soon his grades lent validation to these concerns, and despite the best efforts of his instructors, he ultimately withdrew from the program.

From here, his life took a dark turn, Stanley now recalled, and the pleasant pulsing serotonin stopped dead in his veins. He shuddered to remember it. Back then, alone in his apartment, he had hatched a battle plan for his life and divided it into two parts: the near goal and the far goal. The near goal was to quickly find a better paying waitering job so he could narrow his working life down to one shift per day. The further goal was to figure out what else he could do in life so he could leave waitering behind altogether.

Through pure effort and a touch of luck, the first goal was reached almost immediately. A new, upscale steakhouse was opening further up Route 4 in Englewood, and as he was one of the first to answer the help wanted sign, he got the position. Now, instead of scraping quarters and dimes off a diner's midnight counter, he was making enough to comfortably pay his bills and then some. He'd be home by eleven most evenings, and even had Mondays off if he wanted them.

Unfortunately for Stanley, this new position introduced him to the secret formula that kept his fellow waiters and the kitchen staff humming through the busy evenings; an expensive powder that everyone from the chefs to the dishwashers would furtively inhale several times per night. His first taste of cocaine, provided by a local boy from Leonia who would one day become famous as a world traveling TV chef, came as a revelation.

Suddenly he was a friendly and chipper guy; this was a brand new Stanley Luskin! His banter with the customers went on longer – perhaps too long sometimes – and this often resulted in better tips. He now had enough pep to take on more tables and make more money. He now had the energy to go drinking with the kitchen crew after closing, and was careless on those late nights walking home from his car to apartment. When his number finally came up and he was mugged not a block from his front door, his stolen wallet had been nearly empty, as most of his money had gone to the wise guy at Satin Dolls who sold him his blow. In Stanley's newly perceptive way of seeing things, he felt proud of his street smarts for not carrying so much cash on him.

Throughout this period, in keeping with the doleful ways of the addict, a state of being he had already attained without yet knowing it, Stanley let things fall away from his non-intoxicated life. It started with his small circle of friends, who had already thinned out through school, careers, relocation and marriage. Few of them had been interested in testing their own street smarts by visiting his sketchy neighborhood. Fewer still were as fond of drugs as he was, so when at home, he was generally alone.

He visited his parents once a week, always on a weekday before the dinner shift. These visits were not easy. From his father's point of view, someone who had the leisure to make family visits during the daytime, when respectable "normal" people should be at work, was a *shonda*, and for that matter, so was his son the waiter.

Such visits required more coke to anesthetize their after-effects, and more after that to amp up for the dinner shift, and even more during the shift to keep up with the crowd, and finally a bit more to get up the energy to drive home "safely." Naturally, all this took a major toll on Stanley's ability to sleep, and he soon turned to alcohol as a nightly solution to slow down what the coke had sped up.

One night, after a particularly busy Friday when he'd been dipping more than usual, he plopped himself into his sofa, turned on the TV and worked his way through the second gram he'd bought for the weekend. As luck would have it, he also had a few joints in the house and he smoked one along with his cigarettes. Before too long, it was time to break out the vodka so he could start getting ready for sleep. A third of the way into the bottle, he noticed that he wasn't getting any drowsier, so he went into his medicine chest and took some Sominex tablets, washing them down with swigs of Nyquil.

He was about to light a second joint when suddenly the sound of the TV stopped. It took him a moment to understand that his hearing was gone. Stanley had never heard silence before, real silence. It was as if all the sounds in the world were just noise, a stuck car horn that someone had finally set right. It was fascinating really; the only thing he could hear was his own pulse!

This sensation quickly devolved into horror as he realized his pulse was racing like a greyhound and he couldn't hear anything else. He glanced in terror across the room to the apartment's only window, which usually caught some of the streetlight. The sick green mercury vapor was in frenzied motion, circling, circling – everything was circling. He had to get up, he had to move! He tried to stand and crumpled to the floor.

He laid there for more than a half hour, wondering if he was dying and if he had killed himself by mistake, or if he needed to call an ambulance. He waited a long time before trying to stand, and though wobbly, he managed to stumble into bed. For the rest of the night, the lights kept circling, even under his closed eyelids, like a hypnotist's coin locking him in a steady state between wakefulness, slumber and death. He tried to sleep, willed himself toward sleep, but it wasn't until the sound of a car alarm down the block proved that he wasn't deaf that he could relax enough to become drowsy. He awoke the next morning with a pulverizing hangover and scabs from a bleeding nose. He downed a cup of yesterday's coffee, washed his face, and seeing himself in the mirror, broke down in tears.

Thank God that time is over, he now whistled softly. How could he have put himself through all that? For what? How badly had he damaged his health, how many times had he put people in danger on the road? For goodness sake, how much money did he throw away every night for the privilege of almost killing himself? What possessed him?

Well, he knew now that it was the drug, the very evil, very addictive drug, not his own failing, and he felt a little better. Just read the newspaper, he thought! Bigger shots than him were crashing just the same way from the same evil drug, but they were able to go to fancy rehabilitation centers, while he, Stanley Luskin, had toughed it out alone and delivered himself from addiction through the only tool he understood: sheer bull effort.

It had been an extremely unpleasant few weeks, but every time his body felt miserable during this recuperation period, he would remember the night when he thought he lay dying, and thus was able to carry on until he was detoxed and sober. This episode of personal strength was perhaps the most positive growing experience he'd ever had.

With the earnings that now stayed in his pocket rather than going into small glassine envelopes, Stanley had more of a platform to enact his plan of leaving the waiter's profession. This came just in time, because his performance at the restaurant had deteriorated appreciably during his self-rehab, to the point of a terse ultimatum from the boss. In the course of these unhappy days, he applied for numerous jobs of many kinds, none of which he was especially suited for, with the predictable result that none were offered to him. He finally ended up in the outdoor furniture department at Bamberger's, selling lawn chairs and patio tables.

One day, a pair of newlyweds showed up to shop for poolside furniture for the house they just bought in Fair Lawn; he knew them both from high school. They would have liked to buy from their old classmate, if only out of compassion, and the commission would have been gratefully received, but eventually they went elsewhere, as most of the shoppers did. For the rest of that day and days after, Stanley felt humiliated, inadequate and lost. These feelings were beginning to repeat themselves, beginning to swallow him up.

As he was earning less money now than he was as a waiter, Stanley was again forced to make decisions. He could take a second job, which seemed pointless. Working two jobs to stay at a subsistence level in a sketchy neighborhood with no prospects? Pointless indeed. On the other hand, he could take his savings and move back home, into his old bedroom in the Empress House apartment with the boiled chicken scent, and then…what? More school? To study what field, and to what end? Perhaps more school was pointless too, if there were no prospects beyond.

That was the problem, dammit. The world expects you to be something more than you want to be. It demands that you be something more, you have no choice, he sighed. You can't just be a waiter or an outdoor furniture salesman and also have a life, not here, not anymore, anyway. But why the hell not? The world needs those people too, doesn't it?

After some weeks of soul searching, Stanley arrived at his next plan. He decided to take a position that had been offered to him but he hadn't yet accepted, with the Riteway Diaper Service in Manhattan. It was a sales representative job that would have him traveling all over the city to hawk diaper laundering services wherever he could sell them.

The commute into New York would have made this job unworkable, but as it turned out, someone he had met and liked from the not-Warhol production happened to be living with four other roommates in what they called a loft rather than apartment, deep in the old city, down near the Seaport. He'd called Stanley not long ago, desperately searching for another roommate to fill a recent vacancy, wondering if he might know someone. As it turned out, Stanley now did. He sold his car, spat a goodbye to his Paterson apartment, packed a rented van with his few things and moved into an unconverted floor-through space off Fulton Street, near the city's fish market.

He had to himself a futon, a single small dresser, a garment rack and a curtain that imperfectly separated his "room" from everything and everyone else. In the evenings, when he got home from his long journeys across the boroughs, he'd heat a cup of ramen noodles and settle back to read a magazine. There was no television and the roommates were all night owls. They liked to go to an old church in Chelsea that had been converted into a nightclub and was the New York hotspot of the moment. Stanley joined them once, but as soon as he realized they were basically there to score coke, he recoiled and never went again. Instead, he generally sat alone in the bohemian loft space, reading old copies of Art Forum and the Village Voice and wondering where he fit in. He realized that he didn't. He wasn't a painter, or a choreographer, or a performance artist. He was a diaper salesman. At least until he was something else.

What else, exactly, was the question, still the burning question. He was no closer to finding himself now than he was back at school, or at the restaurant, or anywhere else. He bemoaned a world that would not make a small allocation for him and then leave him alone to enjoy a simple life in peace and dignity; would not provide a niche for him to live quietly and contentedly.

He was not ambitious and never had been, and he did not feel this to be a character flaw, as so many others had admonished. What was this ceaseless ego need, this obsession with personal accomplishment? What is it that drove people like his roommates to live in raw cold water flats with mice and no walls and a makeshift bathroom – all so that they could make sculptures that nobody saw, or compose music that never got played, or write poems seemingly for each other? Did they care about their futures at all, as he did? What was so holy about these endeavors that they could engulf entire lives, consume them completely, essentially define the person?

Who spoke for him, he wondered, someone like him, who had no great drives and no exceptional talents? The world is an enormous place, he thought, but is it so really so small after all that there's no room for those who don't seek fame, or fortune or power, or sex, or any of the other things they say people are driven by? In school they taught us life, liberty and pursuit of happiness. Sometimes happiness isn't freedom *to*, it's freedom *from*, he sighed. Don't we have a right to that? The right to be unexceptional. To be unremarkable. The right to be *ordinary*. The snooty sarcasms he'd heard in college about living an unexamined life made no sense to him at all. The unexamined life, he felt, could be a life saver.

These dense thoughts were inadequate for the evening's entertainment, so Stanley decided to turn in early, as much from boredom as from the fact that tomorrow's first sales call would be in deep Brooklyn, in the growing orthodox neighborhood of Borough Park. He would have to get up early to make the 9AM appointment and once done with that, he'd try to find a kosher deli for an early lunch. While he was there, he might even ring up his sister Esther. He hadn't seen her in almost three years.

The sales call ended on a promising note. The community representative let Stanley know that his local constituency indeed needed many diapers, but they distrusted the newfangled disposables as perhaps having harmful materials, in addition to being much too expensive. Stanley pitched his heart out, and receiving a smile and friendly handshake, left with the air of a salesman who thinks he's already closed. Exiting the building onto Ft. Hamilton Parkway, he was in a light mood for a change. A few moments later, while strolling the main thoroughfare, a strange new emotion shot through him. There was nobody here but orthodox Jews.

If you looked up or down a residential block, took away the cars and changed the architecture only a little, you'd think you were in Mitteleuropa, who knows when or where. This sight fascinated Stanley, he'd never seen anything like it. For the next hour, he walked wide-eyed all over the neighborhood. Women in headscarves shot tandem strollers past him in every direction. All the men wore the same black and white outfits, as if teammates on some cosmic neighborhood varsity squad. Store signs were written in Hebrew and Yiddish, using words he had only ever seen in his father's folded copies of *The Forward*. When he finally chose a deli that looked promising for lunch, he felt completely at home and his food tasted like pure comfort. This was shaping up to be a good day.

He found a pay phone and called his sister Esther. She was surprised to hear from him and delighted to learn that he was nearby in the neighborhood. Why don't you come over now? she asked him. There was no good reason to say no, other than his general discomfort with the life she had chosen. Not much older than Stanley, she was already a mother twice over. He was not at all observant and she was a *rebbetzin*.

Esther's parents had been as unaccepting of their daughter's path as they were of Stanley's thus far. This unhappy truth owed to post-traumatic pathologies that were easier to analyze than endure, with the unfortunate result of markedly fewer visits with the grandchildren than would otherwise be assumed for such people, carrying such back stories. The idea of an impromptu visit from her baby brother, whom she hadn't seen in years, moved Esther in a shade of feeling she could hardly recall. When she got off the phone, she went to the kitchen to prepare tea and a babka.

They hardly recognized each other. "You've gotten so big," she said with a voice that nearly cracked. "And so have you," he answered, touching her pregnant waist. She giggled; it may have been years since she'd done that. Seeing her younger sibling in his cute corduroy blazer sent a Proustian rush of the "old country" through her, as she remembered a graying, faded place where she'd sip Dr. Pepper on the stoop and watch the boys play stickball while John Lennon asked plaintively if she'd want to know a secret.

"Come into the parlor, my big grown up little brother, come in, I am so happy to see you, *Baruch Hashem*." Me too," said Stanley, not without some emotion, before clumsily adding his own *Baruch Hashem*.

It was an unlikely reunion, but it quickly engendered more visits, many more. Stanley soon found himself invited for Shabbat services, and while he was practically a gentile to the congregation, he was treated with sensitivity and respect as the brother of the rabbi's wife. Esther invited him for dinners – "You've gotten so skinny from eating that *chazerai*, come at least to have a kosher meal and be with your family." Soon these became regular events, where he met the *machatunem* and close friends. One night, his brother-in-law asked him point blank why he chose to live aimlessly in the gentile world and not rooted with his own people? Stanley couldn't come up with an answer that didn't sound ridiculous.

In time, Stanley moved to Borough Park, and soon the community representative that didn't end up ordering the diapers found him a job in the shipping department of a camera and electronics retailer. Here, he kept track of incoming mail orders and marked in a ledger when they were shipped to customers. As there were usually only a few dozen mail orders in any given week, the work was not particularly taxing.

A few weeks after starting the job, Stanley began wearing a white shirt with black slacks to work, like everyone else, and after a while, he showed up for the first time with a *kippah* pinned to his crown. With his steady position in hand, and having begun Torah study as well, it was not very long before members of the neighborhood felt comfortable mentioning their daughters. Soon after that, he was introduced to Aviva. She and Shlomo Luskin were married a year later.

All's right with the world after all, thought Shlomo, gazing at his baby daughter as she opened her eyes. Look how well everything ended up, *Baruch Hashem.*

• • •

NEXT YEAR IN PATERSON

The titanic uprights of the Delaware Memorial Bridge loomed as pitiless border guards to another world, which indeed they were for Fradel Gittler, who eyed them with anxiety and resignation as she passed underneath. She was on the move again, they all were. She and her husband Henryk, now grimly focused at the wheel, and Morton, their eleven year old in the back seat, who lowered his magazine long enough to admire the civil engineering. Only Jacob, their college boy, was missing. Fradel had never stopped moving from place to place, she sighed. Not once since she was a girl. Always from place to place and now it was happening again. Maybe. Probably.

They were headed from New Jersey to Tappahannock, Virginia, a sleepy burg in the Tidewater country, where they would spend the next few days at the only motel in town. From there, Henryk and Fradel would begin the search for a house, maybe even in nearby Richmond, where they and their boys would make a home and begin their new life. Work at the textile factory in Paterson where Henryk had labored for the past twelve years had dwindled to only faint signs of life. These days, most of the orders at Empire Woven Labels were being fulfilled by a converted factory below the Mason-Dixon line, opened the previous spring to capitalize on low rural wages and promiscuous tax abatements meant to bring manufacturing into the state.

Ever since then, Henryk had been on a punishing schedule of one week per month "in the south," a seven hour drive that always took much longer. Eventually, the bosses at Empire let him know that they valued him very highly and would like to keep him on, even promote him, but regrettably, the company's Paterson facility would soon be closing. They hoped he'd be open to relocation and the significant opportunity they were now offering him, which was to become the floor manager at the company's remaining plant, located deep in an unincorporated patch of King and Queen County, Virginia called Walkerton, with a population of about four hundred souls.

At the close of the 1960s, the expiring life of industry in Paterson was by no means limited to Empire Woven, or to textiles, or even Paterson itself. Despite his frantic searching, Henryk could find no takers for his skills at the other factories in the area, or those even further away, in the undeveloped woods of Boonton and Whippany. After a week of turndowns everywhere he could think of, he had to break it to Fradel that the family had little choice but to move. By then, Henryk had rationalized that it was probably for the best. But that night, Fradel sobbed herself to sleep.

*

She had never stopped moving. As a young girl in Oradea, she was hardly older than Morton when she was sent to live with a distant aunt and uncle in Budapest. Her father had emigrated to America, where he would theoretically send for the family, but they never heard from him again. She left home to live in an alcove and cot that was called a room, to work in her uncle's bakery from before dawn until the daily wares were sold, and to be lorded over by two older cousins who treated her like a bumpkin servant. This unhappy period did not last, worse was yet to come.

When she was seventeen, she was deported with four hundred thousand Hungarian Jews to Auschwitz, where she miraculously survived for three months before being herded by cattle car to the Stutthof camp near Danzig. There she received her prisoner tattoo of 51306 and survived another year, in the face of sadistic cruelties that distinguished that hellscape from the ruthless efficiency of her previous Golgotha. As the Russian front drew closer in the final days of the war, she was marched west with the other prisoners to Stalag II-D in Stargard, dodging yet again the capricious hand of fate, which might announce itself at any moment through a club or pistol. When the Germans finally fled Stargard, she hid in the latrine for fear of the soldiers of the Red Army, whose reputation preceded them and was in this instance, at least, mercifully undeserved.

From there, Fradel went west again, with the others who were liberated, finally ending up in a displaced persons camp in Landsberg am Lech, Bavaria, with five thousand other survivors. Here she regained her weight and her teenaged beauty finally had a chance to blossom, catching the eye of more than one refugee. One in particular played forward wing for the DP camp's soccer club. Having noticed Fradel from the field, he made dashing goal runs to impress her, which had immediate effect, as she'd never had a boyfriend and no one had ever lifted a finger to impress her about anything. When the dashing forward wing scored the winning tally against the Foehrenwald squad, he pointed at her, smiled broadly and winked.

Whether it was fate in the best sense of the word or something less than the best, it wasn't long before Fradel was carrying a child by Henryk Gittler. The parents knew each other hardly at all, but a birth was a blessed thing, especially now. Every pregnancy was life itself, literally, and under the circumstances, the most dearly won transcendence. The young couple was instantly married, and precisely nine months after his fact, Jacob was born.

When the war was over, the U.S. Displaced Persons Act was signed, reluctantly, by President Truman, who lamented its "pattern of discrimination and intolerance wholly inconsistent with the American sense of justice." Despite the fact that some 90% of the Jewish refugees were initially declared ineligible for immigration, the Gittlers were approved the following year to enter the golden land.

They were eventually shipped to the gritty industrial town of Waterbury, Connecticut, where Henryk would begin work in a textile factory. He had informed the Hebrew Immigrant Aid Society that this was his pre-war trade. That his actual experience consisted of one teenaged summer spent unloading trucks mattered little to anyone. Soon enough in Waterbury, Henryk acquired the skills to navigate the warp beams, heddles, harnesses and shuttles of the great looms, and to coax their most fruitful productions.

All of this seemed providential to Fradel, who praised God and kept the holidays and the sabbath. She'd emerged from the lowest depths of physical and psychological existence to a new life in America with a husband and son and her own home, rented and meager as it was. She was safe, she was free. For the first time, she was in a place where she needn't be apprehensive of her Jewishness and chaperoned by fear, though she was understandably slow to these realizations and reflexively shied away from strangers of all kinds. While she could not speak the language yet, she bought books and began to learn. There were other Jews in this American city, even some survivors like her. Her trauma slowly receded, slipping by inches into the past.

But God had not intended for Fradel to stop moving, not yet. In 1955, two apocalyptic hurricanes, one immediately following the other, swelled the nearby Housatonic and Naugatuck rivers with biblical floods. The waters rose thirty feet above their banks and sped through the streets of Waterbury and the surrounding towns, killing many dozens and wiping out hundreds of homes and businesses. The family huddled throughout the deluge, praying in the dark for God's protection. When they were finally able to leave their building, they found that the factory where Henryk worked was destroyed, along with many others. There was nothing for them now.

In desperation, Henryk reached for a business card he had been given by a traveling salesman, who had asked him to hand it to his boss, but Henryk had forgotten to. The card touted a factory in Paterson, New Jersey that produced woven labels, the types of which were sewn into clothing. Henryk called the man on a flimsy pretext that he quickly abandoned, and soon asked point blank if there might be work at his factory for an experienced man on the floor. As it so happened, the U.S. garment industry had recently begun to add fabric care labels to items of better apparel, and it would soon be the law of the land to include one in every piece. Work was booming. Yes, they could certainly use an experienced hand.

And with that, Fradel was on the move again. In no time, the family found its way to a boxy third floor apartment on Southard Street in one of the most densely populated cities of her new land. No available movers could be found in Waterbury to bring their few sticks of second-hand furniture south. They bought beds for themselves and Jacob, and the Jewish Family Service donated a table and chairs, and even a small couch.

Fradel hardly had time to say goodbye to the few people she had met and liked in Waterbury. Now she and the family were among strangers again, not knowing anyone at all and barely speaking English. She breathed a sigh of relief that they were not homeless, but still stared out the window at the violet evening star and wondered if this bustling place, filled with so much unfamiliarity, would finally be her home.

From this inauspicious beginning, the family made steady, if unspectacular, lives for themselves for a dozen years, *keneine hora*. Fradel was eventually re-connected with cousins in nearby Brooklyn who had also survived the war; suddenly there was some family again. During these 1960s, the city of Paterson hosted a thriving population of nearly thirty thousand Jews. Fradel and her family were no longer alone. Their synagogue's congregation had other survivors like them, with whom they became close friends, celebrated births, Bar Mitzvahs and weddings, played *rummikub* and poker, baked cakes and worked bingo. They were together a community, small and singular as it was, living peacefully and contentedly as Jews in the freest country on earth. Theirs was a unique species of American success story that might ordinarily have been called a happy ending. But now that ending was over and there was only another beginning again. The Gittlers were headed south again. Further south than last time, much further.

"Wait. Who are you?" inquired a curt, imperious voice. Fradel nearly jumped from her skin; there was nobody here. She grasped Henryk with one hand and held Morton back with the other as they entered the foyer of Lowery's Seafood Restaurant, the only place in town still open for a meal at the end of their long day's drive. In the dark vestibule, lit only by the glow of a lava lamp, the terse question raised nearly forgotten hackles on the back of Fradel's neck. The demand came again, louder, visibly unnerving her: "Who are you?"

"It's just a bird, ma," laughed Morton, "Look, it's a Mynah bird. They're some of the best talkers." The boy walked over to the cage, barely visible in a corner of the dim ambience, and tapped on it. "Who are *you*?" he asked in return. The bird eyed its visitor warily before declining an answer. Instead, it began loudly cackling "Welcome y'all!" over and over and would not stop. Even after the family was seated at their table, they could still hear the bird outside until someone finally covered the cage.

The next day, the family drove ten miles from the motel to the factory where Henryk would now be plying his trade. It was a bleached old building in weathered shape, with drooping wooden sheds and the bones of a generator atop a loading dock teeming with lichens and ivy. It sat astride a country road that had only recently been paved by the county. About a mile before their destination, the Gittlers came across a committee of black vultures gathered on the asphalt, greedily ripping at roadkill and only reluctantly lumbering away at the approach of the oncoming Cutlass. Henryk assured Fradel that these large birds don't go after humans, or anything that was alive. There was no need for this warning. She had seen them feasting on roadkill before, back during days she had worked hard to forget.

There was nothing for Fradel or her boy to do at the old factory, of course, except wait for dad's workday to be over. Nothing to do but sit in the buggy heat and wonder if this would finally be her last transition, the last move, as it were. Henryk of course had been resigned to the relocation, but the boys had both been surprisingly welcoming. For young Morton, there might be grassy playgrounds and little league games, maybe even a dog. For Jacob, the first Gittler to attain higher education, the move spelled career opportunity. He looked forward to learning the textile trade from his father and, in time, expanding the Empire further. It all seemed positive for everyone. Fradel gamely concluded that what was best for her family must also be best for her.

At the end of the long, buggy day, Henryk drove the family back to the motel and instructed Fradel and Morton to put on their dressy clothes. As a gesture of appreciation, the bosses at Empire were treating the Gittlers to dinner at the stately Hotel John Marshall in downtown Richmond. Built in the extravagant, heedless styles of the roaring twenties and opened the day after the great crash of '29, the opulent structure was billed as the finest hotel in the south. Presidents, and even Churchill had dined there, and now the Gittlers would too.

As Henryk tentatively inched the car forward toward the hotel's officious bell stand, a uniformed valet motioned him forward with increasing exasperation. His impatient waving quickly ignited a flare of nervous agitation across the front seats that could almost be felt out loud. Fradel didn't understand the man's hand signals either, and never having seen anyone outfitted as a 19th century cavalier, wondered if the family wasn't already being stopped by a police or military official, for some infraction that they may or may not be guilty of, which would be determined solely at the discretion of the unsmiling man now instructing them to pull over.

At that moment, her eyes saucered at the sight of a second man in uniform sternly approaching her door, motioning for her to get out of the car. Shrinking in her seat until the figure was at her window, Fradel could only see the gleaming double breasted buttons and the striped cuff ornaments that must surely be some insignia of rank. The hackles stood up on her neck again, bolder this time, rising in volume as the impatient cuffed hand finally opened the door and motioned for her to get out. She was soon face to face with a fresh-faced teenager smiling amiably, bidding her welcome, and to her boy in the back seat, welcome y'all.

It was the quietest meal the family ever spent. Everyone was petrified into silence. From the way the maître d' pronounced their name when reviewing their reservation, to the moment their chairs were pulled out and ostentatiously dusted off by a pair of somber Black men in servant uniforms, eyes cast to the floor, this was a previously unimagined world of castes, hierarchies and manners that the Gittlers could only guess at. The men in servant's garb were soon followed by others just like them, silently orbiting the honey-voiced and decidedly not-Black waiter, whisking crumbs, switching napkins, placing finger bowls mistaken for tea, and confusing everyone by taking silverware away between courses.

When the bill was presented, it was of a sum that neither parent believed possible for a single meal, and Henryk turned white to see it. He growled at Morton for having ordered dessert and prayed that the restaurant remembered that a company credit card number had already been provided in advance. Whether it was or wasn't, Henryk still had to explain this unusual arrangement to the waiter, which he was flustered to do in his imperfect English, especially when diners at nearby tables stopped to observe the confusion and the people with the funny accents. Finally the maître d' was summoned to the table, who assured Mr. Gittler that the bill had indeed been taken care of, and please, let us assist you in getting you and your family to your car, right this way please.

*

The next day, the family drove into Richmond again to meet real estate brokers and browse houses for sale, and to also visit a synagogue, which they assumed as a first point of sanctuary. They saw charming brick bungalows with garages and back yards – these would be remarkable upgrades for the family – that were located near well-regarded schools for young Morton, whom the sunny realtor patted on the head. One home in particular appealed to them and had real promise, but when they were shown the back yard, they saw that it adjoined the rear of the New Covenant Baptist Church, which happened to be having a potluck, and whose members were now joyfully singing a hymn about "Power In the Blood." The Gittlers collected the broker's card and silently drove to their next destination.

Congregation Beth El was the oldest synagogue in Richmond, with a pedigree dating almost from colonial times. In the antebellum years, it had switched to the Reform movement, adding an organ and a choir, and these days, extended its works of *tikkun olam* into programs for orphans, the indigent and the elderly. As Fradel and Henryk approached the building, they could hardly believe their eyes at the immense Greek colonnade of the grand neo-classical building. They hadn't seen such a beautiful shul since before the war; their hearts reflexively softened.

They had made no appointment, so when the receptionist asked their business, they couldn't exactly say, other than they were moving here and were Jewish, and this was the temple that had been mentioned to them. The flustered woman soon returned with a cheerful administrator who greeted them with "Welcome, or welcome y'all, as we like to say here." After some brief chitchat, she routed the Gittlers into a magnificent sanctuary, as grand as any they'd known back in the old world, with astonishing stained glass and a soaring dome that recalled Constantinople. Suddenly the air was filled with the ecclesiastic sonorities of choir practice, with thick church-like polyphony accented by throbbing low notes from a huge pipe organ. The group stood silently to listen. As their guide smiled beatifically at the liturgical outpouring, Fradel and Henryk clutched each other as if it were Sunday mass. Once in the car, they shuddered at the *goyishe* synagogue and wondered if they could ever feel at home there.

*

On the final day of the trip, the family checked out of the motel and drove once again to the factory. There, Henryk would attend to some final details for a few hours, after which the Gittlers would start back home. Fradel and Morton re-assumed their positions from yesterday; she with a straw hat on the mildewed loading dock, he throwing rocks at unseen targets. It was hot and boring and Fradel had enough of sitting there doing nothing. She called Morton over and suggested they go for a walk. The boy tossed his remaining ammo and the two of them headed down the road, beyond where the factory was, past dense growths of pines, birches and cedars, for perhaps a half mile until the pavement ended in a fork of unpaved dirt roads.

Noticing a large snapping turtle ambling up the path to the left, Morton quickly moved to observe it at close hand. He was about to touch it, maybe even pick it up, but then he saw its fearsome beak and thought better of it. Instead he followed it forward as Fradel stopped to pick a wild strawberry the size of a pearl. They strolled down the dirt road for a while longer. Morton was transfixed by the sounds of so many birds, so many insects and frogs, so much wildlife. What else must be in those woods, he wondered? Fradel was delighting in her boy's curiosity and picking the other wild berries she found as they walked. Their perfumed sweetness reminded her of happy days as a child, when her mother would walk with her down paths just like this one, many eons ago.

Both of them heard it at the same time. A car was approaching on the dirt road, hidden by many curves up ahead, approaching, coming closer, inexorable. Fradel looked behind her and realized she couldn't see the main road anymore. The hackles returned and began pulsing in alarm. Morton looked up with no great concern until he saw his mother stiffen like a quail in the brush.

The car was very close now, and he moved his mother to the side of the road when they saw it. It was a pickup truck driven by two bearded men wearing military camouflage. Mounted behind their heads was a fearsome rack of rifles. On the bed of their muddy vehicle, an enormous white tailed buck was sprawled, its tongue lolling in shocked disbelief at its untimely fate, its black marble eyes fixed intently at Fradel's, as if imploring her assistance. The men crawled to a stop and paused for an agonizing moment in the shadows before jointly stepping out of the truck.

Her blood ran completely cold. Even the hot, humid air around her turned ice cold. Everything was cold and frozen, and there was nothing Fradel could do. She instinctively reached for Morton but he was now standing in front of her, in a protective stance that no doubt looked comical as the men approached, though they did not smile. Sinewy men, men with dirty hands and military clothes, armed with guns, and now they were stepping toward Fradel and her boy. They sized up the woman and the situation as the woods became quiet. In those seconds, a thousand scenes flashed through Fradel's mind, unspeakable sounds and images that had almost been forgotten, but now flooded back all at once, turning her blood frozen cold. She stared at her confronters in paralyzed silence.

The taller one, the driver, looked down at her impassively and asked, "What y'all doing here?" Fradel could not find it in herself to answer. He waited for her to speak and stared at her until she would, but she wouldn't. Receiving no reply after an excruciating pause, he turned to the boy. "What y'all doing out here?" he repeated.

Despite the macho pose he'd been affecting, Morton had no illusions of being a hero. But in his innocence, he didn't sense any need. The guns and the dead deer were not scary, they were interesting. The two men did not seem to be overtly threatening. "We were just taking a walk," he explained. "Here?" the man asked, with mild disbelief. "Yes, we were just walking," he repeated. "Did we accidentally go somewhere we shouldn't?"

The men slowly looked at each other and then back at the mother and child. "No, you're fine," the second man allowed. "You all right?"

Morton didn't know what he meant. Did they look like they weren't all right? He looked at his mother and silently agreed that she didn't look like she was all right. She hadn't moved a muscle since the truck arrived within view. He turned back to the two interlopers and replied, "We're fine. We finished our walk anyway, now we'll go back to the factory up the road. My dad's there waiting for us."

Satisfied with this response, the driver paused before nodding his head and drawling, "Don't see too many walkers around here. Thought y'all might need some help is all. If you're all right, you take care now." The men climbed back into their truck. As they pulled away, Fradel's eyes were still locked on those of the dead buck, which only recently had met up with these same two men.

Fradel grabbed Morton's arm and wheeled him around, back in the direction from which they came. They had walked only a few quick steps before she stopped and caught her breath. Realizing now that she might be frightening the boy, she crouched down and said to him, in a firm, conspiratorial tone, "We not moving here."

She repeated this phrase intermittently all the way back to the factory. Once there, she motioned for Morton to sit by the loading dock while she went inside to confront Henryk and inform him of same, that we not moving here. The boy was alone for perhaps ten minutes before both parents stormed out of the factory and motioned him into the car. The couple switched to Yiddish, but this couldn't mask their quarrel, which rose in volume until it broke into stony silence, whereupon it would quickly burst open again, with anguished shouting and eventual tears. Only one English phrase occasionally poked through – we not moving here.

Henryk drove them back to the motel and informed the desk that the family would need another night. Then, after shoving a five dollar bill into Morton's hands, his seething parents dropped him off at the only movie house in town, telling him they'd pick him up at the end of the show. They sped away, leaving Morton to stare at the box office window and the lurid poster for a grindhouse movie about a vicious motorcycle gang. The picture was rated R, meaning he should theoretically be denied entrance without an adult, but the cashier silently took his money and slid a ticket through the slot.

Once inside, the boy came upon a half-filled theater, taking in the last of the coming attractions. Only then did he notice there was a balcony, which was generally his preferred location. Turning toward it, he noticed there weren't many open seats. Most of them were taken by Black and Latino patrons, who through former law, lingering custom or perhaps prudence, sat in the upper rear.

Morton didn't know what to do. He was eleven years old, by himself in a dark, strange place with people staring at him, and an adult movie had started to run. He hurried into a seat near the exit and watched goggle-eyed as Bruce Dern and a gang of savage toughs brutalized innocent people for no reason, and as Melody Patterson, the alluring Wrangler Jane of his F Troop afternoons, posed fully nude for an artist, and at length. In eighty four minutes, Morton was exposed to more violence and sex than he had ever known, and upon leaving the theater, was never fully the same boy. His parents were waiting for him outside in the car, where his mother was still shaking her head to the mantra: "We not moving here." But she was wrong.

*

In the end, they did move there. Fradel's wishes were not honored. Perhaps it was the pull of the family's opposing wishes, or because there was no real alternative to speak of. But to her chagrin, and eventually her resignation, Fradel would soon be on the move yet again. It wasn't long before the Gittlers had migrated into a white shingled house on a quiet block in the suburbs of Richmond. There was a small back yard with a cherry tree where the orioles loved to build nests. Henryk and Jacob enjoyed an easy father and son commute to the Empire factory each morning. Morton was enrolled in a nearby school, close enough to walk. It all seemed like another happy ending. But here, Fradel's troubles began.

Everything had worked out fine, for only a while. The *tsouris* arrived in the first year, when one day Morton was sent home from school with a black eye and a gash that required three stitches. He was the only Jewish boy in his class, one of only two in his entire school, and as such the target for a diverse and equitable community of tormentors, including his gym teacher, who singled him out mercilessly for additional laps and pushups, and found ways to steer him to the front rows of dodge ball. There was no cure for it, no answer, no other place the Gittlers could afford to enroll their boy. They could only teach him strength, perseverance and faith, and on these topics they had reliable real world experience.

In the second year, there was bad news from the bosses at Empire. Orders had slowed, profits were down, and the southern factory with its outdated machinery wasn't turning out to be so much cheaper than the old shop in Paterson. They had to trim payroll, and Jacob was laid off, along with several Mexican loom workers who lived in mobile trailers behind the plant and would now have to move on, somewhere. And while it was indeed cheaper for Empire to produce woven labels in the south than in the north, the company had discovered it was cheaper still to make them even further south, in Mexico or Trinidad, for example, where it was exploring the takeover of yet another old factory. Though still faint, the writing was on the wall.

Early in the third year, there arrived an official looking letter addressed to Jacob, and when Fradel pulled it from the mailbox, she thought she felt her hand turn numb. It was from the U.S. Selective Service, which had recently begun a lottery system for draftees to serve in Vietnam. Everyone knew what was in the envelope before it was opened, as the family nervously scanned the unlucky birthdays in the newspaper after every drawing. Jacob's number was up, and he was hereby ordered to report for induction into the armed forces of the United States.

He would likely be sent to southeast Asia, to fight a country that his parents had barely heard of and couldn't find on a map, for a cause that they didn't even know, much less understand, and maybe they'd be losing their first born forever. This was the darkest moment the family had ever spent. In the old country, Henryk's uncle had been drafted – stolen really – to fight the Bolsheviks when they unleashed the Red terror on unfortunate Poland. He'd been captured and sent to the gulag, and was never heard from again. Fradel's grandfather had been similarly impressed into the Romanian army during the first great war, and had miraculously survived, but he'd returned home a sickly and shaken man, hobbling with an oaken leg. She could still remember the pathetic clack on the floor as he struggled from room to room.

With overwhelming sadness but unconditional support, the family stood behind Jacob's decision to escape the draft and emigrate to Canada. There he'd find refuge among the tens of thousands of other American men who had also found sanctuary there. Fradel pleaded with him to visit when he could. She didn't understand that he never could, that he would be arrested and worse if he tried, and that he had no idea when he'd see the family again. Everyone cried until daybreak. In the morning, Henryk drove Jacob to the Greyhound station, where he boarded a bus for Montreal, twenty five hours and a lifetime away.

By the fourth year, the writing on the wall was highly legible, though there was little Henryk could do about it. Running a short-handed factory with aging equipment wasn't good business, the bosses had concluded. Eventually, they informed him that if they didn't close down the Virginia factory, the company would go have to go under. Henryk asked where Empire Woven Labels would now make its goods if they closed their remaining factory? They told him that for months they had been sending orders to their plant in Trinidad, of which Henryk had been only lightly aware. The bosses asked half-heartedly if he might be interested in moving to Trinidad? By the end of the next month, Henryk got a pink slip, a letter of recommendation, and a good-will payout of two hundred dollars.

From there, he drifted from place to place as he tried valiantly to provide for his family. He found work in another textile factory not far away, and when that one closed too, he found another. By this time, he'd made numerous connections with buyers and sellers of woven goods from several eastern states, and his English had become passable enough to find work a salesman, where he cold called potential customers. It was, unfortunately, a difficult transition to a monotonous desk job consisting mostly of annoyed rejections, and he came home in the evenings tired and defeated. As depression was not widely recognized, understood or treated in those days, not even by a wife, Henryk found little solace, and after dinner would bury himself with television before drifting off to sleep in his chair.

In the fifth year of their sojourn, Morton graduated from high school and prepared himself for college. He had waited intently for this moment; it was finally his chance to get away. To go someplace at last where he'd no longer be attacked or denigrated for being a Gittler, or for being smart; a cosmopolitan place where he could grow in peace, as an equal. He applied to schools all over the northeast, as far away as he thought he could go while still in range for family visits. He was offered a scholarship to study statistical science at Drexel University in Philadelphia, and by September of that year, Fradel and Henryk, for the first time ever, were genuinely alone together.

*

It would have been altogether too lonely for them, especially for Fradel, had it not been for a young family that had recently moved next door. They were also transplants from the north, more or less, with two young boys and a girl. Suddenly there were children in Fradel's life again. The kids took to her like the grandmother they missed back in Delaware, especially their youngest Jeremy, who was a budding artist and would often come by with a sketch pad and crayons. He even began painting with her, and Fradel held a brush for the first time since she was a girl. The Campania family quickly became indispensable members of Fradel's day to day existence, the first Christians she had ever become close with. Their loving kindness shattered long-held preconceptions that had never seen the light of counterexample, and made them intimate friends and the best of neighbors to the two remaining Gittlers.

Soon there would be only one. By now, Henryk had become much older than he really was. A host of ailments grew more debilitating. Emphysema from years of breathing microscopic fibers; arthritis from decades of manual labor;

gastric and sleeping problems brought on by stress and poor diet; the list was unremitting. Henryk had faithfully saved what money he could for many years, and always kept his life insurance policy up to date. It wasn't much, but it came in handy when he passed away from a coronary event. Jacob could not cross the border for his father's funeral. Morton had to ask at Temple Beth El if there weren't some Jewish volunteers to help make up a minyan. In the end, the Campanias sat shiva for Henryk.

*

Following his college graduation, Morton accepted a position with a federal agency in Washington. He chose this path in part for its easy trips to visit his mother, which he undertook faithfully at least once per month. He worried about her; she had become frail and occasionally disoriented after the loss of her husband, and the companionship of the Campanias notwithstanding, she spent every day by herself. She needed to get out, to be with people, to have conversations and company. They talked it over, and Fradel agreed that getting out of the house once in a while would probably do her good.

During his next visit, once he fully overcame her wailing that "her son was putting her in a home," Morton drove his mother to the Beth El Senior Center. The friendly receptionist quickly put Fradel at ease, and the lounge-like lobby of the guest area felt to her like a fancy hotel. Soon, a young volunteer brought a tray of tea in small glass decanters. Fradel remarked that this was how tea was steeped and served back in the old country, which piqued the intern to ask where that was. "It was Romania," said Fradel, "But really it was the Hungarians. You would not know," she chuckled. "You are too young."

The young woman smiled back at her and asked if she

meant Transylvania? "Yes, that's what it was!" Fradel laughed. "How you know this?"

The intern, whose name was Tina, cheerily explained that her own father had come from Ukraine, having narrowly passed through the iron curtain in the aftermath of the war. She knew all the nationalistic back and forth about Transylvania, and said her family joked about it whenever there was a vampire movie on TV.

Fradel laughed again and patted the girl on the hand. "This is a good one," she affirmed to the others, pointing her thumb at the beaming intern. Her supervisor nodded agreement, and asked Tina to take the Gittlers on a tour of the facility. Fradel hooked her arm inside Tina's and the three of them ambled happily down the spotless linoleum hallway.

Passing through the lobby, they came across a large table with an architect's model of the new Montefiore Center for Senior Living, which was under construction a few miles away, and would soon replace this current facility. Fradel had never seen anything like it before – so realistic, so beautifully detailed, down to the tiny trees and cars! "How do they make such a thing, my God," she exclaimed.

"In real life, the new buildings will look just like this," explained Tina. "At least they're supposed to," she added wryly. As his mother cooed over the sprawling model, the elegance and scale of this planned facility gave Morton a needed flash of security. She couldn't stay by herself forever, he thought.

The capper to the day, and it was a wonderful day, came when a program manager described the center's activities that Fradel could enjoy – arts and crafts, movies, lectures, music, sabbath services and more – and informed them that the center ran a free shuttle service for seniors who live in the area. They'd pick her up and drop her off; Fradel wouldn't even have to drive here! This provided disproportionate relief to Morton, as his mother was not a good driver. By the end of this first happy outing, Fradel and Tina were bonded like sisters, and a next visit was already planned. When mother and son pulled up in their driveway, Fradel leaned over and kissed her son before breaking into tears.

*

Buoyed by this new lease on life, a peaceful and happy year went by. Fradel was shuttled to the senior center three and sometimes four days a week. She found friends there, as Morton had hoped, and a community she'd been missing ever since moving "in the south." Outside of this new circle, she'd never really adapted to her life in Dixie, beyond the safe perimeters of her own back yard and that of the Campanias. When she went grocery shopping, she rarely spoke to anyone, remembering the time a produce clerk snickered when she shyly asked if the store sold *kelarib*. It took a befuddled manager a few tries to finally understand that she meant kohlrabi, and no, they'd never had that here.

One day, a police car pulled Fradel over on her way home from the drug store. The flashing beams, mirrored aviators and officious demand for her documents produced a pulsing anxiety that never fully left her psyche. She had been driving too slowly and erratically, said the officer, who would now be reporting her name to the state, which would soon require her to re-take her driver's test and obtain a new license. Fradel shook behind the wheel all the way home, convinced that the government was taking her driving away when she'd done nothing wrong, nothing, and because *mein mazel*, she had come into contact with the spiritual or actual offspring of a Gestapo officer. "A hundred percent a Gestapo," she mourned.

So eventually, Mrs. Campania did all the grocery shopping for Fradel, just as Mr. Campania changed the light bulbs and window screens. Their oldest boy cut the grass, and their daughter helped her in the garden, while their youngest Jeremy taught her to paint and sketch from memory. He even came with her to the senior center every now and again. When Tina saw how well Jeremy energized the sleepy residents during the arts and crafts hours, she asked if he'd be interested in coming in regularly, as a sort of instructor. Soon, Jeremy was a volunteer at the Beth El Senior Center, having taken the first step in his path as an art teacher, which became a guiding passion for the rest of his life.

*

One day, as if by a miracle long overdue, there was stupendous news. The new President of United States, a peaceful man and a southerner to boot, was granting a full amnesty to the thousands of young men who had avoided the Vietnam draft. Jacob could come home at last! Morton excitedly called him with the news, which was no news to Jacob, who had been following the story closely in Canada. The brothers would finally see each other again. Fradel would finally reunite with her boy!

The excitement was, unfortunately, too much for the moment, and the miracle was tainted by fate, which finally caught up with Fradel. Upon hearing news of the amnesty on the television, she had bolted from her sofa to the telephone in the kitchen, where she promptly tripped, fell and blacked out. It was sheer luck that Mrs. Campania had rushed next door to make sure Fradel heard the news on TV, where she found her friend lying unconscious. An ambulance was called, and while Fradel's vitals gave cause for optimism, the fact remained that she had hit her head, and there was the possibly of a fracture.

Morton had barely hung up with his brother when Mrs. Campania phoned him with the awful news. He called Jacob back and advised him to make urgent travel plans. The older brother said he'd need a day or two to arrange an emergency passport and would call when he had flight information. Morton advised him to fly to Richmond instead of Washington, and that he'd be driving to Virginia himself that night. He arrived at his parents' house close to midnight, slept in his old bed, and prayed.

The next morning, Mrs. Campania saw Morton's car in the driveway and invited him for breakfast with the family. The kids had grown up so much since Morton had moved away, they were practically adults now. All were heartbroken by Fradel's fall and let him know they were praying for her recovery. Jeremy in particular had something he wanted Fradel to have in the hospital, a talisman of sorts. It was a small figure he had made, the size of a sparrow, painted in ochre and gold. It was a token of Saint Raphael the Archangel, who heals the sick. Morton was touched by the gesture. He told the family he'd be off to the hospital right after breakfast, maybe Jeremy would like to bring it himself? The teenager hurried himself to go.

The doctors had encouraging news. They had determined that there was no fracture, though there was cranial trauma and swelling they'd need to keep an eye on. Fradel was still unconscious and might remain so for another day, but she was resting well and she'd soon be leaving intensive care. The prognosis so far was as good as one could hope for. Morton and Jeremy were overjoyed by this news, which softened their disappointment over not being able to see Fradel. Come back this evening, the nurse advised, and while she may not be awake yet, you'll at least be able to be with her.

During the drive home, Jeremy asked Morton if he would mind stopping briefly at the Beth El Senior Center. The staff had heard the terrible news about Fradel this morning and they'd be relieved to know she'd be all right. "She talks about you so often, everyone there must feel like they know you already," said Jeremy. "I'm sure they'd love to finally meet you,"

"I didn't realize I'd be a topic of conversation, but I guess I should have," chuckled Morton." Sure, I'd be happy to. I wonder if that young woman I met, I think Tina was her name, is she still there? My mother really liked her."

"Still there? Tina's a program manager, I know her very well," grinned Jeremy. She's the one that brought me on to teach arts and crafts. Hey, you're finally getting to see your hometown again! I'll bet that'll be a kick." Morton screwed up his brow. "You mean here? I don't remember it being a kick."

"Not here. *Megem ofus*, as your mother calls it. Actually her pronunciation was so cute that we all adopted the name – *megem ofus*." Morton squinted and shook his head, "I really have no idea of what you're talking about."

Jeremy shot a puzzled smile before suddenly closing his eyes and frowning. "Aw sugar." Pursing his lips and pondering for a moment, he eventually reasoned out loud: "Well… I think it'll be okay." Morton kept his eyes on the road as he asked what, exactly, would be okay. Jeremy directed him to take this exit and then a quick left.

The staff at the Center was overjoyed to hear the news about Fradel. Tina hugged Jeremy and even Morton, saying that she felt like she'd known him for years. "I guess that's not surprising," she grinned. Your mother has been such an inspiration to me, like a second mom. I'm so happy she's going to be all right."

"He's never heard of the *megem ofus*," laughed Jeremy. "I forgot it was a surprise and I mentioned it." Tina's eyes broke into a smile. "Oh, well…I wouldn't worry about it, I'm sure she'll forgive you. Fradel's full of surprises right? Should we go see it?"

"See what? Morton finally asked, not without some impatience. Tina patted him on the arm and smiled at Jeremy. "Come on."

The three walked down the hall to an empty activity room. Once inside, Morton noticed a group of tables joined together in the corner, covered with plastic shower curtains. Jeremy steered them to these tables and smiled at Tina and Morton. Theatrically clearing his throat, he announced, "We have the honor to present to you now, Fradel's *megem ofus*. It's a work in progress, but we're all pretty proud of if already. She said she wanted to surprise you with it when it was done, but really, who knows if it will ever be done? And under the circumstances, I don't think she'd object to you getting a sneak peek. Plus I blew the surprise anyway," he laughed.

He pulled the sheets away and Morton gazed on in amazement. Sprawling before him was an enormous model, or diorama, or something in between, of downtown Paterson, New Jersey. "She supervised the whole thing," said Tina with pride. "She and Jeremy started out with just one building, then the other seniors saw it and they all got hooked, and now look at where it's gone!"

Morton was flabbergasted. The work in front of him was shockingly detailed. Signs and marquees of the old Paterson were artfully painted on tiny buildings made from poster board and shoe boxes. Striped drinking straws became stately Doric columns. Toy soldiers were mounted atop pedestals of bingo chips and became solemn memorial statues. Paper towel tubes were the smokestacks of the nearby factories. There was even a train track, pulled from some grandchild's detritus, with a curving termination at what looked to be the edge of old downtown. Tina and Jeremy smiled at Morton's stunned silence. He finally stammered, "This is incredible. She never said a word about it. What did she have to do with this?"

"Well, it was supposed to be a surprise," laughed Tina, winking at Jeremy. "She would often reminisce to us about Paterson. For hours sometimes. She said it was the one place in her life where she was the most happy. None of us knew anything about it of course, but she knew it all, brick by brick, just about."

"We spent a lot of time sketching and painting from memory," added Jeremy, "And these were the memories that came up most often. One day, here in the crafts room, she started 'building' what she said was the city museum. It's that one over there," he said, pointing to a former ice cream carton. "Then the other residents got a kick out of it and they started making pieces for it too. Then everyone started adding to it, they made quite a little community! Think of your mom as the city planner, she directed the whole thing from memory. We've been working on it for, well, for almost six months, wouldn't you say?" "At least," corrected Tina.

"One day we called it Fradel's magnum opus, which she loved but couldn't pronounce," Jeremy chuckled. Every time at crafts day, just about, she said she wanted to work on the *megem ofus,* so that's the name we all adopted. Look at all this detail! We learned all about your hometown from her memory. That big box over there, that's Meyer Brothers, she said she loved to shop there." Morton swallowed the lump in his throat. "She did, she really did love it. I remember going with her many times. There and Quackenbush." Tina pointed to another box and said "That's Quackenbush, we just haven't made the sign yet."

The ingenuity of this makeshift city was mesmerizing, and brought back uncountable memories for Morton, piling on all at once. A glittering rhinestone hairclip framed the marquee of the jewel-box Fabian theater. A large peanut in the shell, mounted on toothpicks and sporting a top hat pulled from a Monopoly set, touted itself as "Fresh Roasted." There was a stately city hall built of poster board and unmatched Lego blocks. A plastic castle, appropriated from a grandchild's princess set, was painted as the armory, with a billboard the size of a playing card offering bingo Tuesday and Thursday nights. In the corner of the table, looming over the city, was a sculpture made of papier-maché that depicted, in gushing streams of blue, green and white, the majestic flow of the great falls. On the opposite corner, in a modest size, was an elegant white shoebox with a golden star of David on the roof that the Campanias had contributed. It was her synagogue.

"I never knew about any of this." was all Morton could say as he choked up. "She never said anything." At this point, he was overcome by the moment and asked where he might sit for a while. Tina and Jeremy brought him to a small visitors lounge and left him alone.

*

Morton turned off the light, closed his eyes and quietly thanked God for the scope and variety of his mercies. His mother had never uttered a word of her longing. He understood with a grimace that *no, of course she wouldn't have*, for fear of upsetting her family. Once Henryk and the boys left Paterson they never looked back, only forward. Only Fradel looked back, and they never knew. Alone among her lifetime of lost worlds, there'd been a place and time that she remembered fondly, exactingly, where she finally had the chance to be rooted, to live peacefully and contentedly among family and friends, and to be happy. That his mother's Shangri-La turned out to be a rust belt casualty five thousand miles from her birth, a place Morton thought they'd gladly left with no regrets, seemed an unendurable irony.

He was hit by a flood of emotions. What would happen to her now? He'd have to take her back to New Jersey for a visit, at least to see her friends again. *Next year in Paterson!* he laughed to himself. But what would she find there?

He didn't have the heart to tell her that her world was gone. He'd kept up with a few pals from the old neighborhood over the years, even visited once. The Jews had all left, just as the Gittlers had. The family synagogue, a welcoming port for so many survivors like themselves, had dwindled and closed, its congregation melting into the suburbs. Another of the local shuls had become a special needs school, yet another a mosque. The grandest temple in the city, the magnificent Art Deco jewel of the Eastside, now stood empty and eroding, a ruin from an ancient civilization.

It had been years now. The kosher butcher was now a halal butcher. Her beauty parlor was a braiding center, and her favorite bakery was now a panaderia. Instead of bingo at the armory, there was professional wrestling. The buses to downtown were no longer strictly safe; for that matter, neither was downtown. In yet another blow to the city, the shopping had migrated to the newfangled indoor malls in the suburbs, leaving behind husks of bewildered businesses. The Gittler's old house now had a chain link fence around its tiny front yard, patrolled by a wary Doberman.

The Jews of Paterson were gone forever. It was a gentle

exodus, with little trace of the hatreds that had emptied Salonica, Pinsk, Mogador and so many other havens of the old world. No one had forced them to leave. This was America, the new world; they had voted with their feet and moved on. Fradel's special place was a ghost. And so, her son realized, was his own.

• • •

THE PERSISTENCE OF MEMORY

No one could say when the connection started, even if someone had guessed that such a thing existed at all. Believed or disbelieved, acknowledged or ignored, fervently prayed for or unnoticed like a passing butterfly, it effortlessly whisked its way through time and space, through centuries and continents and oceans. It would tarry in waiting for its expected perfect completion, and if it found none, move on to a next waiting stop, indifferently into the future or past, or the other side of the world. It would often come agonizingly close to its ultimate form and then just miss, ever so slightly, whereupon it would move patiently to the next possibility, lying in wait, restlessly scouting, always scouting, always seeking its final culmination.

There had been uncountable numbers of these near misses since the seventh day, effected by acts of men or acts of God, but these did not bend or break the connection, which emanated from God and slipped through these diversions with liquid ease. It had very nearly completed itself in Egypt, swooping through the multitudes in frantic migration across the desert and sea. It had located its one half and then the other, but they were lost in the tumult of the Exodus. It seemed again like its work might be done in Antwerp, three millennia later, but the ship, hopelessly overloaded by the cruel hands of the Reconquista, sank near Gibraltar and never arrived. It sought its fulfillment from Morocco to Peking, from Oslo to Cape Town, in cities and in *shtetls*, mansions and *lager* barracks, old people and young. It had no strategy for success, other than to complete itself, which it would, someday, as surely as the sun rises. From there, if it could, it would propagate itself and begin the process again.

*

The lemon tree outside her bedroom window was casting its familiar moonlit shadows, and Dalia stared at them wakefully as they swayed across the ceiling. She was anxious and knew that she shouldn't be, it was bad for her, bad for everyone. She should have been in the peaceful, contented slumber of afterglow, as Eitan was beside her, but her mind felt spitefully caffeinated. This after she had long ago cut out coffee and tea, and worst of all chocolate, in an effort to safeguard her body against caffeine and other pollutants, from hindrances. She and Eitan had been married for six years, and for almost three years trying to start a family. In all that time there had been no sign of a family to come, not with coffee or without, and her mind was well accustomed to nocturnal anxieties on this topic. Which is why they had no trouble keeping her up yet again.

They had tried everything, even patience, which was what most of the doctors had advised. After all this time, how patient would they have to be? she wondered, having long lost faith in this remedy. Persistence was deemed the better solution by family and friends, advice that found much favor with Eitan. But over the course of time, it became difficult to distinguish the grace of making love from the labor of making a baby. The unsuccess of the latter cast a pall over the former, and the couple became painfully aware that these two were not necessarily the same thing.

Then there were the long stretches when Dalia would carefully monitor herself and her ostensible fertility, picking just the right diet and the right mood and time, all to no different effect than if she'd never bothered with her notes and charts. The same dedication was expected from Eitan, who watched his food and drink, did his exercises, and introduced new and perhaps promising positions he'd seen in a translated Kama Sutra. The result was always the same. Truthfully, a little less than the same, after each time of the month.

The couple was thoroughly examined and tested and no doctors could isolate the problem; there was nothing wrong with either of them. An attempt was made at in vitro fertilization, but the procedure did not succeed, for reasons that were explained as chance, as opposed to skill or any deficiencies. The couple was welcome to try again, and the doctors encouraged it, but the disappointment was too profound for Dalia to undertake it again. At least not yet.

*

On the other side of the world from Rehovot, in a smoky corner of the old Gil Hodges Lanes in Mill Basin, Brooklyn, Isaac Shindler was marking down one score while contemplating another. He was on a double date, he and Heather McDonald, the object of his visualizations, along with his pal Jeff Waxman, who together with his steady Diane Salerno could always be counted on for support in these matters. The thunderclaps of the alleys hindered the conversation, which turned out to be fortunate, as Isaac was finding there just wasn't much to talk about with Heather. He didn't yet realize that she felt the same way. When the games were over, he walked her home, and she rewarded him with a kiss that politely and clearly conveyed finality. Which was fine with both of them.

It was all very frustrating though, Isaac sighed, as he trundled down Ralph Avenue to his bachelor studio. How long can this go on, after all? He was nearing thirty, the age when most of his friends had long ago sown their wild oats and settled down, some here in Brooklyn, others to greener pastures in Long Island and Westchester. The neighborhood was changing, but Isaac was staying the same, and it gnawed at him.

He had even turned his life over, re-dedicated the whole damned thing not long ago at all, having been given a second chance to live after a frightening bout with cancer. He had come through the ordeal all right, but only in the present tense; there would be no more Shindlers to follow. Not after six weeks of radiation therapy.

The doctors had prepared him for this outcome, and prior to his treatment he was advised to visit their fertility center, where they'd collect his potential children and guard them in cold storage until they were ready to meet their mother. He had dutifully undergone these sessions, suppressing a blush as he was handed a cup and a folder of magazines by the nurse, walking quickly past the averted eyes of the women of the waiting room, nervously gathered there for related mercies made possible by modern medicine.

Isaac's survival from that most pitiless of diseases was, in a way, a bargain that was foisted on him, one that he had no choice but to accept. Yes, he would live on, but he'd also be the end of his line, a reality that cut him deeply. As an only child and second generation to boot, he was he last link of his family, the final ember of a branch of the Shindlers burned away by the Shoah and washed up as flotsam on the American shore. With so much family lost, it had been up to him to bring it new life, as so many other Shindlers had done forever, back in the old world.

He had always regarded this inevitable regeneration as a cosmic mission that had been assigned to him, his larger reason for being on this earth. One day in the future, he and his other half – yet to be determined – would present the gift of posterity in honor and remembrance of those that came before and had been tragically lost. Not coincidentally, this poetic culmination would also proffer a definitive middle finger to Hitler and all he stood for.

Thanks to said modern medicine, there was indeed a possible future for more Isaac Shindlers to come as they safely slept in cryogenic storage; at least a fractional chance. But for that plan to work – and it didn't always work – there needed to be the second party, a mother to be, the other half to be, and the absence of such a person, near or far, was beginning to feel like a lingering truth. He just wasn't hitting it off anywhere, nothing seemed right, and the weight of the misfires was becoming cumulative. He had always been popular with the girls, but none of it ever proved durable. As a serial monogamist, he moved from one relationship to the next like a bumblebee, hopping clumsily from flower to flower.

Tossing his shoes in a corner and slumping into his couch, he was glad he'd be going away soon, because he really needed to clear his head. In fact, his whole life needed a serious reset and he was open to anything – anything. That was the rationale behind his upcoming trip. He hadn't been to Israel since his Bar Mitzvah year, when he'd accompanied his parents on whirlwind visit to find their few remaining relations. He barely remembered any of it, not least because no one besides his parents could speak English. This trip would be another experience completely and he couldn't wait to go. Who knows what might happen to him there.

*

When Dalia heard from her mother that her American cousin Isaac was coming for a visit, she didn't have much reaction. She barely remembered such a relation and had to be reminded that they had met at all, if only for an afternoon, back when they were thirteen. He must not have made much of an impression, thought Dalia, but she took the news cheerfully. She'd get to practice her English, and she didn't receive many visits from America, or anywhere else these days. In fact, these days were becoming very much the same of late, and she didn't know how much longer she'd want to go on without doing something, maybe anything, to change them.

She had considered the possibility that she and Eitan might never have children together. That happened sometimes, didn't it? If it did, would her marriage last? She wasn't sure. She had now been married for six years to a man who might have been an ideal member of a family of three or four, maybe even five. But for a family of two, there was a lot of space available that Eitan wasn't built to inhabit.

He had tried, to his credit, to go with her flow, attempted to share her interests these years, but it was an obvious effort and against his grain, because the plain fact was that he was a salt of the earth kibbutznik in heart and soul. He was not skillful or practiced at conversation, or needful of it; he'd read few books or cared to, thought little about world events or much at all outside of his immediate purview. They had married young. To a cultured twenty one year old like Dalia, who was a teacher after all and from a family tree with multiple scholars, all lost, Eitan had been a handsome, grounded, complementary opposite. But now, to her chagrin and a bit of her shame, Dalia approaching thirty was starting to feel that the man she married was perhaps a better match for her once upon a time.

*

Isaac sipped his fragrant Yemini coffee with deep satisfaction; he had never tasted anything like it. The newness of the sensation perfectly matched the utter novelty of just about everything else he'd come in contact with during this, his first trip to the holy land as an adult. Jews everywhere! Everywhere Jews! The bus drivers, booksellers, bank tellers, falafel makers, business suits, construction crews, the pretty girls in miniskirts; all of them Jewish! The ordinariness of it was extraordinary, overwhelming. It was all out there in the flesh and incredible to him; irreducibly real, actual, unapologetic, a world made of Jews, by Jews, Jews who were home at last, free at last. While he spoke no Hebrew and had never been observant, the energies of Jerusalem moved him profoundly. It touched him in the way Paris reaches those lucky enough to live only for beauty; a sacred spot on this earth where an elemental human yearning is understood, honored and fulfilled.

As his bus approached Rehovot, Isaac leafed through the handful of photos his mother had asked him to bring to his distant Aunt Dorca, who was Dalia's mother and Isaac's host for the next two days. He didn't know who any members of these yellowed portraits were, perhaps Dorca might, and in any case, she'd appreciate the mementos. As Dorca spoke no English, Dalia was home with her to greet Isaac, which she did warmly and fluently. Though they hadn't seen each other in fifteen years, they instantly recognized each other and a frisson of familiarity went through both of them, like the overtones of a bell separated from their fundamental pitch.

The next day, Dalia took her cousin to the Mediterranean at Palmachim Beach, wild and undeveloped. It was a crystalline, blindingly beautiful day, so routine in that part of the world, and on a weekday morning, the shore was nearly empty. Dalia had prepared a picnic lunch, and at Dorca's insistence, Isaac brought along the gift he'd presented to the family, the nicest bottle of Bordeaux he could afford in Tel Aviv. This unusual offering had elicited a smile of confusion from Dorca – *who brings a fancy vayn as a guest, does he think we're shikkorim?* Dalia, however, grasped the sentiment behind the American's gift and looked forward to tasting it. She'd never had a glass of French wine.

They stripped to their bathing suits and sat themselves on the tideline, the gentle water lapping just over their waist. The turquoise sea was exactly as it had been described to Isaac, warm as a bath, intoxicatingly placid. He moaned and sighed at the pleasure of it, prompting Dalia to smilingly ask if there were no such wonderful beaches in America? Of course, he laughed, although the ones he knew were the shores of the Atlantic, which were usually cold and turbulent. If you wanted a beach this gentle, you'd need to go south, like down to Florida.

This prompted Dalia to mention her older brother Menachem, who had moved from Rehovot to Miami some five years ago. He was apparently doing quite well as a contractor and electrician, Dalia said, he even had his own business already. "Do you remember him?" Isaac did not, nor did he know that he had a cousin in Miami. "I'm thinking of going to visit him soon," said Dalia. "I may even think about moving there."

Hearing this surprising statement, Isaac looked at her quizzically. She was genuinely beautiful, he suddenly realized. It was an arresting, complex beauty, so much more than the way she looked, which would have been more than enough. The gentle slopes of her neck gave way to sculpted shoulders, achingly feminine, flowing into arms like palm leaves, past a lithe body almost exactly his own size, all of which sent a considerable quiver through his various inner selves. He could feel her warmth from a few feet away, even though the blazing heat; could pick out her scent, subtly present, somehow plant and animal at once. He was ashamed to have any such thoughts, not matter how fleeting, about someone who was a married woman and a cousin besides.

He reflexively thought to avert his eyes but didn't, because he saw that she was gazing at him too and did not look away. Their eyes locked together in a moment of sublime tension. "I've never told this to anyone," she said softly.

Dalia looked back at him beyond her five senses, because now her own body was quavering too, ever so slightly. He was a handsome man, regardless of his funny American look, notably the hair, which reminded her of African athletes she'd seen on TV. She took in his tapered, olive-skin body, a swimmer's body, with graceful, muscular limbs and shoulders; all unsheathed, save for the scant European-style trunks which were all the rage in Tel Aviv but still seemed a bit risqué for Rehovot. More than a bit. Her eyes nervously moved past him, out toward the sea, but this took genuine effort, and as she stared off in the distance, she knew all the while that he was still gazing at her. She turned back to his eyes and the moment was electric again. The spark of it made them both turn away.

"That's a big decision," was all that Isaac could think to say. "What would you and Eitan do there?" "I would not go with Eitan," she said, even more softly. "I would go by myself."

*

Time is not a well-understood member of the material world. We owe it to our landsman Einstein for conceiving of it as a fourth dimension, a useful theory that at least opens a door. But even this daring insight only hints at what we can perhaps never know. Time can move quickly or slowly, laughing at clocks and counters, but infinite mutability only hints at its essential power. Time's duration is less mattering than the content it carries. A year of long division can be forgotten in days, but a fleeting glance can last forever. Five minutes of a dripping pipe may never be noticed by anyone, but the same minutes of an open firehose plays havoc.

*

And just now, time was indeed playing havoc with both Dalia and Isaac, rushing through them both with a roaring, deafening firehose of visions and emotions. It should be obvious that none of this was audible, visible or even namable, but both of them felt the great force nonetheless; intensely, as tangibly as they could touch the water at their waists. After a moment – which might have gone on for seconds or hours, given the wry playfulness that time was presently enjoying – they realized they'd been locked into each other's eyes. The intense attraction, to use a paper-thin word that only hinted at the infinite depth of the connection, was deeply palpable, almost impossible to restrain.

Isaac was in the midst of an outer-body vision of himself cosmically intertwined, body and soul, with this gentle, beautiful woman that was looking downward at the sand with a tiny smile that might have been shyness or regret, or, if he dared to believe, invitation. In the rush of the firehose, he knew he *could* dare to believe, he could. He could gladly undertake a lifetime of diligent, joyous work to fully interpret and comprehend that tiny smile, do all he could to nurture it and make it grow, to earn even greater smiles, permanent smiles, and live within them, sleep within them, raise children under them. It was a flashing revelation of a greater happiness then he'd ever imagined, and as it coursed through him, his staggered mind eventually rose to its feet.

Omigod, what was he thinking? How close of a cousin is she anyway? *Distant enough.* But she's married and she's in Israel. *But she might move to America and might come alone.*

In the firehose of emanations, these thoughts flickered like fireflies, finally nestling into a glowing, tree-shaped light, its branches heavy with luminous, poetic, impossible realities that might actually be possible. Isaac felt drunk, and he hadn't yet opened the wine.

Dalia was having an outer body experience as well, or more precisely, inner body, as the firehose washed through her more quietly, yet no less furiously. She could feel herself, almost literally, lying contentedly in the arms of this relative stranger who feels like he's known her all her life. She can feel his warm breath on her hair, feel herself softly kissing his chest above his beating heart, and then looking past him to see their son and daughter peeking over the bed at them, giggling, hoping to not wake *ima* and *abba.* In this vision, which was more vivid than any dream she'd ever had, she felt a weight drop from her body and her psyche, an unbearable weight. She felt fetters unclasp, and actually saw her disembodied spirit free itself and float above her, intertwining with Isaac's into the shape of a spinning hexagram, then another and another, as they dissolved into the sun-drenched clouds overhead.

Trailing far behind all this, her mind finally caught up and asked how close of a cousin is he, anyway? *Distant enough.* But he's in America and I know so little about him. *You know more than your mind can tell you, is this not obvious?* Dalia felt lighter than air, lighter than the substance of the firehose. She suggested they open the wine.

*

The two of them talked and drank wine and soaked in the sea until dusk. Over the course of the day, the firehose receded to a gentle lapping, in sync with the Mediterranean. Neither of them dared say anything overt about it, though they had no doubt the experience was mutually felt. Instead they exchanged oblique conversational gambits that were couched in cousinly interest and concerns.

This was clue gathering of the most delicate kind, because in the present and most relevant dimension of all, Dalia was still married to Eitan. The elemental question, of course, was her admission that she might emigrate without him. Isaac could find no diplomatic way to ask why she'd consider this kind of radical transformation – precisely the kind of yank-the-tablecloth move he'd been open to himself since being declared in remission and getting a clean bill of health.

She told him that she and Eitan had been trying for years to start a family and it just wouldn't come to be. And if there was no family possible for her, then she'd rather have a different life than the one she saw for herself here in Rehovot with Eitan. Her brother would help her make a new life in America, just as he had done for himself.

It all made sense, her story did, and Isaac would be lying if he was not, on some level, hoping she'd never stay in an unfulfilling marriage. He was vulnerable in this hope, because the firehose had easily soaked through a heart that was still fragile from its recent close encounter with mortality. It was then that Dalia told him the most interesting thing he'd heard about her, even though everything about her had been infinitely interesting already. She lifted her cup of Pauillac and smiled at him and said, "You should know that your cousin is no longer Dalia. My name is now Liora. It has been changed. It means my light."

"Why did you do that?" asked Isaac, toasting her plastic cup. Dalia – Liora – explained that she and Eitan had tried every method they could think of to have a baby. The doctors could find nothing wrong, it was a puzzle. They tried the fertility treatments, the in vitro process, none of it worked. Finally, a friend of hers had suggested that there were kabbalist rabbis who believed there is a spiritual tie between one's given name and their soul, and to change one's name is to change their destiny. What did she have to lose? "I'm not sure I believe it myself," she smiled, but I thought why not give it a chance? So many things in life depend on chance, do they not?"

*

They said they'd write to each other but they never did. They never got the chance. A little more than a month after his Israel trip, which had restored his spirits and his rejuvenated his hopes, Isaac got a phone call from his aunt in Toronto, another distant relative of Dorca and Dalia, that is, Liora. She barked through the phone with less than her usual good humor.

"You stinker you! What did you do, eh?" Isaac could think of no reason for this outburst, other than he hadn't called her in a long while, was that it?

"You make big trouble, *nah*? Mister, what did you do?" The news was incredible. Dalia – never mind the *narrishkeit* with her name, spat his aunt – was pregnant. Happily pregnant. But suspiciously pregnant.

"*Years* they are trying and nothing for her, and you come and go in one day and *pffft*, eh? Where did you go? You *stinker* you! Now what you do, eh?"

Isaac tried to stifle his laughter but was unsuccessful. The absurdity was potent enough, but there was real joy running through him too. Liora would finally complete herself, he was so happy for her, he could feel her vibrations, sense the bell overtones again right now, just thinking of her.

He explained to his aunt that nothing at all had happened between them, a story which took several retellings before a grudging acceptance. He reminded her that any children of his that he *might* have one day yet to come are currently living in cryogenic storage, and not in Rehovot. And yes, he was completely aware that Eitan was a trained soldier who knew how to handle a gun. Finally, for punctuation, he added that nonetheless, maybe he was such a stud that he could get a girl pregnant by simply talking to her.

"Big shot," huffed his aunt. "Funny guy. *Shtendik der modne bokher.*"

*

The following spring, Liora gave birth to twins. This was hardly unusual in and of itself, and in fact not unusual at all, given all the fertility treatments. What was somewhat unusual about Levi and Eliana was how completely different they were in almost every way. The boy was dark and olive skinned, while his sister was pale and red headed, like Eitan. He was wakeful and restless and loathe to sleep, while his sister happily acquiesced to bedtime and every nap. As they grew up, these personalities would solidify and become who they were; the restless one and the stable one, the daring one and the measured. They were brother and sister of course, and twins, but for all the world to see, they may as well have come from two fathers.

*

While they were all elated at this turn of events, the rebbes could not agree on whether this particular connection had finally achieved its purpose, or whether it had merely come close again, which was even more interesting to contemplate. As one might expect of such a distinguished celestial convocation, there were spirited debates supporting both cases, with many variants in between.

Speaking as the party who had actually changed the mother's name, Rebbe Eliyahu felt that perhaps it was too soon to tell. What if there was a latency period, so to speak, when the connection could rest and restore itself, bestowing *some* of its blessings in the meantime, while perfecting itself for another generation, yet to be born? Then it could be *both* a success achieved and a success *yet to come.*

This provocative theory garnered hearty murmurs of interest, and the celestial voices congratulated its speaker on his subtlety before returning to the joy of their spirited debates.

• • •

GLOSSARY

Yiddish, the language of Ashkenazic (European) Jewry since the Middle Ages, was (and still is) spoken with many local variations. While most Yiddish vocabulary is based on an amalgam of medieval Hebrew and German (with a smattering of Aramaic, Slavic and Romance languages), many words are derived from specific cultures or regions. Pronunciation often varies by geography; I have tried to keep these inconsistencies alive through spelling and implied phonetics. Hebrew is denoted with an (H), Yiddish with (Y), all others as written.

-- RG

Aliyah – Literally ascent; modern usage is the immigration of diaspora Jews to Israel (H)

Bagrisn – Welcome, greetings (Y)

Bar Mitzvah/Bat Mitzvah – Coming of age ritual; Bar is for a boy, Bat for a girl (H)

Baruch Hashem – Blessed be God; often said before or after a conversational sentence (H)

Bashert – Literally pre-ordained, colloquially a soul mate (Y)

Bialys and pletzels – A bialy is similar to a bagel, pletzel is a flatbread similar to focaccia (Y)

Blanquito – Colloquial and derogatory Spanish term for a white person; "whitey"

B'nai B'rith – Literally children of the covenant; a global Jewish services organization (H)

Bubbes – Grandmothers (Y)

Boychik – Kiddo, pal, buddy; an affectionate term for a male (Y)

Chazerai – Food that is awful, unclean; also describes something worthless (Y)

Chutzpah – Audacity, nerve; can be either complimentary or disparaging (Y)

Davened – Prayed (Y)

Doboks – A uniform worn in Korean martial arts, such as Taekwondo

Doji – Formal Japanese name for a karate uniform

Du redst Yiddish? – Do you speak Yiddish? (Y)

Este ardiendo – It's burning (S)

Farshteist – Do you understand ? (Y)

Farzenishe kinder – Monstrous children (Y)

Filles lache – Loose women, French

Fressing – Snacking; implies heavy snacking (Y)

Ganav – Hebrew for thief; *goniff* or *gonev* in Yiddish (H)

Gay gezinterheit – Literally go in good health, colloquially, *go right ahead* or *good for you* (Y)

Gluss teh – A glass of tea (Y)

Golem – Mythical man-made protector of Jews, brought to life by a spell (H)

Goyim – Plural noun for non-Jewish people (H)

Goyishe – Adjective for something non-Jewish in substance or spirit (Y)

Groisse machers – Literally big makers, meaning "big shots" (Y)

Guy avek – Go away (Y)

Halakah – The system of legal and ethical principles that guides daily life within Judaism (H)

Haimishe – Literally homey or familiar, colloquially Jewish or Jewish feeling (Y)

Haftorah – a reading from the Prophets, chanted by Bar/Bat Mitzvah candidates (H)

Hola pendejos – Hello assholes (S)

Ich kum – I'm coming (Y)

Ima and Abba – Mom and Dad (H)

Kalooki – A card game, a version of rummy from Europe

Kapo – Jewish concentration camp inmates who were forced by the Nazis to serve as stand-in guards (Y)

Keneine Hora – An expression of gladness or praise, typically affectionate (Y)

Keren Ami – A charitable fund (H)

Kibbitz – To engage in casual conversation, sometimes in an unwanted way (Y)

Kibbutz – In Israel, a communal community that lives and works together; plural *kibbutzim* (H)

Kibbutznik – A member of a kibbutz collective (H)

Kippah – Hebrew word for skullcap worn by Jewish men; *yarmulke* in Yiddish

La revanche des berceaux – Literally the revenge of the cradles; a high birth rate (F)

L'chaim – Literally to life; heard as a toast during a gathering or celebration (H)

Machatunem – In-law families (Y)

Magen David – The shield of David; six-pointed star symbol of the Jewish people (H)

Mazel tov – Literally good luck, colloquially an expression of congratulations (H)

Mein mazel – Literally my luck (Y)

Mensch – Literally a man, colloquially an upstanding man (Y)

Meshuginah – Crazy or nonsensical, an insulting adjective, also used as a noun (Y)

Minyan – A quorum of at least 10 Jewish adults required for certain religious services (H)

Mishpochah – Immediate extended family (Y)

Moishe Maccabee – Maccabees were ancient Jewish warriors; Moishe is Yiddish for Moses

Modeh Ani – A Hebrew prayer said each morning, expressing gratitude for another day

Nar – A fool (Y)

Narrishkeit – Foolishness, nonsense (Y)

Nishtik – Puny, worthless (Y)

Nu – Multi-purpose word most closely translated as "so" (Y)

Oy, azoy a mechiah! – Oh, this is a pleasure! (Y)

Pinkt Fakert – Exactly the opposite (Y)

Pisher – Literally someone who piddles, colloquially someone young or inexperienced (Y)

Plotzer – To plotz is to burst or explode (Y)

Rebbetzin – The wife of a rabbi (Y)

Rummikub – Euro-Israeli tile-based game combining elements of rummy and Mah Jong

Sabra – Literally a cactus fruit, colloquially a Jewish person born in Israel (H)

Schmaltz – Rendered chicken fat (Y)

Schnorrer – A moocher or layabout (Y)

Schvartze – The color black, also a Black person; often but not necessarily derogatory (Y)

Shepseleh – Diminutive of a sheep when derogatory, a lamb when affectionate (Y)

Shikkor, Shikkurim – A shikkor is a drunk, shikkurim is the plural (H)

Shiva – Mourning period following a Jewish burial (H)

Shmeggege – A foolish or worthless person (Y)

Shtendik der modne bokher – Always the funny guy (Y)

Shtetl – Until the Holocaust, a Jewish village, primarily in Eastern Europe and Russia (Y)

Shul – Literally a school, also used as a word for synagogue (Y)

Tateleh – Term of endearment for a young boy (Y)

Tikkun Olam – Literally means repair the world; human acts that radiate harmony (H)

Traif – Literally unkosher, colloquially a word for bad or unfamiliar food (Y)

Tuchus – A person's rear end (Y)

Tsouris – Trouble, distress, a cause for suffering (Y)

Tu carro – Your car (S)

Tzedakah – Literally righteousness, colloquially charity (H)

Yarmulke – Yiddish word for skullcap worn by observant Jewish men; *kippah* in Hebrew

Yerida – Literally descent; the opposite of *aliyah*, used for Jews who emigrate from Israel (H)

Yeshiva – A private school focused on traditional Jewish education (H)

Yeshive bucharim – Yeshiva students (H)

Yiddishe kup – A Jewish head; colloquially a Jewish brain (Y)

Yiddishe seichel – Jewish brain or mind (Y)

Zaddik – A righteous man (H)

Zei gezunt – Be well, used as a farewell (Y)

Zonot – Immoral women, harlots (H)

• • •

ABOUT THE AUTHOR

Ron Goldberg

Ron Goldberg's creative life has spanned all manner of old and new media, including film, music, television and the internet. As a technology columnist for New York Newsday, his work was read nationally via the Los Angeles Times Syndicate, and his multimedia producer's "bible" has been courseware on four continents. An early web pioneer, he was a tech correspondent for one of the first online newspapers in the U.S., and a co-architect of the web's first broad-scale portal for consumer electronics. Turning to the world of make-believe, Ron's fiction was first published by the Jewish Literary Journal in 2024.

A son of Holocaust survivors, Paterson native and longtime New Yorker, Ron now lives in Los Angeles with his wife Brenda.

www.rongoldbergauthor.com

• • •

9 7 9 8 2 1 8 6 5 5 3 7 2